by Marguerite Yourcenar

NOVELS AND SHORT STORIES

Alexis ou le traité du vain combat, 1929;
in English, *Alexis*, 1984

La nouvelle Eurydice, 1931

Nouvelles orientales, 1938; revised edition, 1963, 1978;
in English, *Oriental Tales*, 1985

Le coup de grâce, 1939; in English, *Coup de Grâce*, 1957

Mémoires d'Hadrien, 1951; in English, *Memoirs of Hadrian*, 1954

L'oeuvre au noir, 1968; in English, *The Abyss*, 1976

Denier du rêve, 1934; revised edition, 1959;
in English, *A Coin in Nine Hands*, 1982

Comme l'eau qui coule, 1982

POEMS AND PROSE POEMS

Feux, 1936; in English, *Fires*, 1981

Les charités d'Alcippe, 1956

DRAMA

Théâtre I, 1971

Théâtre II, 1971

ESSAYS AND AUTOBIOGRAPHY

Pindare, 1932

Les songes et les sorts, 1938

Sous bénéfice d'inventaire, 1962;
in English, *The Dark Brain of Piranesi*, 1984

Discours de réception de Marguerite Yourcenar à l'Académie Royale belge, 1971

Le labyrinthe du monde I: Souvenirs pieux, 1973

Le labyrinthe du monde II: Archives du nord, 1977

Discours de réception à l'Académie Française de Mme M. Yourcenar, 1981

Mishima ou la vision du vide, 1981

Le temps, ce grand sculpteur, 1983

ALEXIS

Marguerite Yourcenar

Translated from the French by Walter Kaiser

in collaboration with the author

Farrar Straus Giroux • New York

Alexis

Originally published in French under the title
Alexis ou le traité du vain combat

Printed in the United States of America

Designed by Cynthia Krupat
Library of Congress Cataloging in Publication Data
Yourcenar, Marguerite. / Alexis.
Translation of: Alexis. I. Title.
PQ2649.O8A7513 1984 843'.912 84–6009

For him

Preface (1963) *Alexis, or The Treatise of Vain Struggle*, appeared in 1929; it belongs to a certain moment in literature and in morals when a subject which up to then had been deemed forbidden received for the first time in centuries its full written expression. Almost thirty-five years have passed since its publication: during that time, the ideas, the social customs, and the reactions of the public have altered, even if less so than is commonly believed; what is more, certain opinions of the author have changed, or could have changed. It was therefore not without a certain anxiety that I returned to *Alexis* after this long interval: I expected to have to make a number of alterations in the text to make it consonant with a world that had itself altered.

And yet, after thinking it over, such changes seemed to me unnecessary, if not downright damaging; hence except in matters concerning a few infelicities of style, this little book has been left as it was. There are two reasons for this, which at first glance may seem contradictory: one is the highly personal character of a confession strictly limited to a milieu, a time, and a land now vanished from maps; a confession, moreover, impregnated with the old-fashioned atmosphere of Central (and essentially French) Europe, in which the slightest detail could not have been changed without transforming the acoustics of the book. The second reason, in contrast, is the fact that this story, judging from the reactions it continues to provoke, seems to possess a sort of relevance, and even usefulness, for some people.

Even though this subject, formerly considered illicit, has now been amply treated and even exploited by literature in our time, thus acquiring a sort of legitimacy, it would nonetheless appear that Alexis's intimate problem is hardly less anguishing or secret today than it was formerly, nor would it appear that the relative ease (so different from true freedom) with which this subject is discussed in certain tightly restricted circles has done anything more than create in the public at large an increased misunderstanding or wariness. It is enough to look around attentively to perceive that the drama of Alexis and Monique continues to be lived out and doubtless will go on being lived out so long as the world of sexual realities remains shackled with prohibitions, perhaps the most dangerous of which are those of language, which bristles with obstacles most people easily avoid or work their way around but upon which the scrupulous and the pure in heart are almost inevitably impaled. Morals, whatever one may say, have changed too little for the central subject of this novel to have become very outdated.

It has perhaps not been adequately observed that the problem of sexual freedom in all its forms is, in large part, a problem of freedom of expression. It seems clear that, from generation to generation, the tendencies and the acts themselves vary little; on the contrary, what changes is the extent of the zone of silence or the weight of the layers of lies surrounding them. It is over the innermost realities of marriage itself, the sexual relations between spouses, that verbal superstition has imposed itself most tyrannically. The writer who endeavors to present the story of Alexis honestly, eliminating from his language formulae which are supposedly decorous but in reality are the semi-timorous or semi-licentious formulae of cheap literature, has little choice except between two or three modes of expression more or less inadequate and often unacceptable. The scientific terminology recently formulated and doomed to become outmoded with the theories that support it, worn away by an excessive popularization which quickly takes from it its virtue of precision, is valid only for the specialized works for which it has been created. Its labels go against the chief aim of literature, which is individuality of expression. Obscenity, a literary mode which has always had its adherents, is a defensible shock treatment if one has to force a prudish or indifferent public to face what it does not want to look at or what, as the result of too prolonged a habit, it can no longer see. Thus, the use of obscenity can correspond to a sort of cleaning up of words, to an attempt to give a kind of clean, peaceful innocence to a vocabulary essentially neutral but soiled and dishonored by usage. Yet such a brutal solution remains an external solution: the hypocritical reader tends to accept the unseemly word as a form of the picturesque, almost as a form of exoticism, a little the way the passing tourist in a strange city allows himself a visit to the slums. Obscenity is soon exhausted, forcing the author who relies on it into excesses which are even more threatening to truth than the understatements of past times. The brutality of language conceals the banality of thought and, with certain major exceptions, is indistinguishable from a kind of conformism.

A third solution may offer itself to the writer: the use of that spare, almost abstract language, both circumspect and precise, which in France has for centuries served preachers, moralists, and often novelists in the classical period as well, as a vehicle for discussing what was termed at that time "the aberrations of the senses." This traditional style for the examination of conscience lends itself so well to the formulation of innumerable nuances of judgment on a subject which is by its nature as complex as life itself that a Bourdaloue or a Massillon resorted to it for the expression of indignation or censure, and a Laclos for licentiousness or voluptuousness. By its very discretion, this decanted language has seemed to me especially appropriate for the pensive, scrupulous deliberations of Alexis, for his patient effort to free himself strand by strand—unknotting rather than breaking them—from the web of uncertainties and constraints in which he finds himself caught, for his modesty which includes a respect for sensuality itself, and for his firm desire to reconcile with dignity the spirit and the flesh.

Like every story written in the first person, *Alexis* is the portrait of a voice. It was necessary to let this voice have its own register, its own timbre, to remove from it, for example, none of the courtly inflections which seem somehow out of another age and already seemed so thirty-five years ago, nor to remove from it any of those virtually suppliant accents of tenderness which perhaps, in the end, say more about the relations between Alexis and his young wife than his confession itself. It was also necessary to permit this character certain opinions which today seem rather doubtful to the author but which retain their value for characterization. Alexis explains his penchants as the effect of a puritanical childhood completely dominated by women, possibly an accurate opinion so far as he is concerned and very important for him from the moment he accepts it, but one which (even if I believed it at the time, and I no longer recall whether I did or not) now seems to me the sort of explanation that tries artificially to place within the psychological methodology of our age deeds which probably go beyond that type of motivation. In the same way, Alexis's preference for sexual pleasure enjoyed independently from love, his wariness of any prolonged attachment, is characteristic of a period in reaction against a whole century of romantic exaggeration: this point of view has been one of the most widespread in our day, whatever the sexual tastes have been of those who express it. One might respond to Alexis by observing that sexual pleasure isolated in this way runs the risk of turning into a dreary routine; even more, that there is a puritanical essence in this attempt to separate pleasure from the rest of human emotions, as if it were not worthy of belonging to them.

As he leaves his wife, Alexis offers as the motive for his departure the quest for a more complete sexual liberty unblemished with falsehood; and certainly this reason remains the most decisive one. Yet it is probable that other motivations are involved which are even more difficult for the departing person to admit, such as a longing to escape from a prefabricated comfort and respectability, of which Monique had become, despite herself, the living symbol. Alexis adorns his young wife with every virtue, as if by thus increasing the distance between her and himself he would find it easier to justify his leave-taking. I have sometimes thought of composing a response from Monique, which, without in the least contradicting the confession of Alexis, would clarify certain aspects of this experience and give us a less idealized but more complete image of this young woman. But for now I have abandoned that project. Nothing is more secret than a woman's existence. The tale of Monique would probably be much more difficult to write than the admissions of Alexis.

For those who may have forgotten the Latin of their schooldays, I should note that the name of the principal character, and hence the title of the book, is borrowed from the *Second Eclogue* of Virgil, "Alexis," from which, and for the same reasons, Gide took the Corydon of his controversial essay. In addition, the subtitle, *The Treatise of Vain Struggle*, echoes *The Treatise of Vain Desire*, that rather pallid work of André Gide's youth. Despite this allusion, there was not much influence of Gide on *Alexis*: the quasi-Protestant atmosphere and the attempt to reexamine a sexual problem both come from elsewhere. What, on the contrary, I find once again on more than one page (perhaps excessively so) is the influence of the profound, moving work of Rilke, which a happy chance brought to my attention early on. In general, we tend to forget too easily the existence of a sort of "law of delayed diffusion," which explains why educated young people around 1860 read Chateaubriand rather than Baudelaire and those at the end of the century Musset rather than Rimbaud. Although I don't consider myself in any way typical, I myself passed the years of my youth in a relative indifference to contemporary literature, partly as the result of my study of the past (and thus a work on Pindar, really quite clumsy, precedes this book on Alexis in what might be called my oeuvre), partly as the result of an instinctive distaste for what one might call modish values. Most of the great books of Gide in which my subject had at last been discussed openly were as yet known to me only by hearsay; their effect on *Alexis* is much less the result of their contents than of the fuss made about them, of the sort of public discussion which focused on a problem up to then examined only behind closed doors, and which certainly made it easier for me to approach the same theme without excessive hesitation. It was above all from the point of view of *form* that my reading of Gide's early books was valuable to me, demonstrating as they do that it was still possible to employ the purely classical form of the novella, which otherwise would probably have seemed both precious and outmoded to me, and preventing me from falling into the trap of a real novel, the composition of which demands of its author a variety of human and literary experience which I did not at that time possess. All this is certainly not intended to reduce the importance of the work of a great author who was also a great moralist, even less to separate *Alexis*, written in isolation from the fashion by a twenty-four-year-old young woman, from other contemporary works with more or less similar intentions; on the contrary, it is intended to lend them the support of a spontaneous confession and an authentic testimony. Certain subjects are in the air at certain moments; they are also in the fabric of a life.

Marguerite Yourcenar

ALEXIS

This letter, my dear, will be very long. I am not very fond of writing. I have often read that words falsify thought, but it seems to me that written words falsify it even more: you know how little is left of a text after two successive translations. Then too, I do not know how to go about it. Writing is a perpetual choice between a thousand expressions, none of which satisfies me, none of which, above all, satisfies me without the others. Yet I ought to know that only music permits a succession of chords. A letter, even the longest, is obliged to simplify what should not have been simplified: one is always so much less clear the minute one tries to be complete. I should like to make here an effort not only of sincerity but also of precision: hence, these pages will contain many erasures; they do already. What I would ask of you (the only thing that I still can ask of you) is not to skip over any of these lines which will have cost me so much. For if it is difficult to live, it is even more difficult to explain one's life.

Perhaps it would have been better if I had not gone away without saying anything—as if I were ashamed, or as if you had understood. It would have been better for me to have explained myself quietly, slowly, in the intimacy of our room, at that hour of dusk when one sees so little that one dares admit almost everything. But I know you, my dear. You are a very kind person. In this sort of account, there is something pitiable which can cause the hearer to be moved; and because you would have felt sorry for me, you would have believed you had understood me. I know you. You would have wished to spare me the humiliation of so lengthy an explanation; you would have interrupted me too soon; and I would have been weak enough to hope that I would be interrupted at each phrase. You have another quality as well—a defect perhaps—which I shall speak of presently and which I do not wish to abuse any longer. I am too culpable toward you not to force myself to place a distance between me and your pity.

It is not a question of my art. You do not read the newspapers, but mutual friends will have told you that I enjoy what is called success—which is to say nothing more than that many people praise me without having heard me and some without having understood me. It is not a question of that: it is rather a question of something not really more intimate (for what is more intimate to me than my work?) but which seems more intimate because I have kept it hidden. Above all, more wretched. But, you see, I am hesitating; every word I write takes me a little further away from what I wanted to express at the very outset. That merely confirms that I lack the courage. I also lack the simplicity. I have always lacked that. Yet life is not simple, and that is hardly my fault. The only thing that persuades me to go on is the certainty that you are unhappy. We have lied so much, and suffered so much from lying, that there really is no great risk in seeing now if sincerity will not restore us.

My youth, or rather my adolescence, was absolutely pure—or what is called pure. I am aware that such a claim always provokes a smile, because it generally indicates either a lack of perspicacity or a lack of candor. Yet I do not believe I am deceiving myself, and I am confident I am not lying. I really am sure of that, Monique. At sixteen, I was what you doubtless hope Daniel will become when he reaches that age, but let me tell you, you are wrong to hope such a thing. I am persuaded that it is a mistake to force oneself to consign all the perfection one is capable of to the memories of one's most distant past. The child that I was, the child of Woroïno, no longer exists, and all our existence is characterized by infidelity to ourselves. It is dangerous for the first of our illusions to be the best, the dearest, the most mourned. My childhood is as distant from me as those nervous expectations one has on the eve of holidays or the torpor of lengthy afternoons when one lies about without doing anything, hoping that something will happen. How can I hope to find that peace again, which I did not even know a name for then? I have renounced it completely, realizing that it never wholly belonged to me. But let me confess at once that I am not even sure I always regret that ignorance we call peace.

How difficult it is not to be unfair to oneself! I said to you just now that my adolescence was untroubled. I believe it. I have often looked back at this rather puerile, sad past; I have tried to remember my thoughts, my feelings, more intimate than my thoughts, even my dreams. I have analyzed them to see if I might not discover some ominous meaning which had escaped me then, and whether I had not mistaken innocence of mind for innocence of heart. You know the ponds of Woroïno; you always say they are like great pieces of gray sky fallen to earth, which then strive to rise up again as mist. When I was a child I feared them. I already understood that everything has its secret, ponds as well as everything else; that peace, like silence, is never more than a surface, and that the worst of all falsehoods is the falsehood of calm. All my childhood, when I think back on it, seems to me a great calm on the edge of a great disquiet which is, in fact, the whole of life. I think back to incidents, too minuscule to recount, that I did not notice then but where I now perceive tremulous warnings—quiverings of the flesh and quiverings of the heart, like the breath of God the Bible speaks of. There are certain moments in our existence when we are, inexplicably and almost terrifyingly, what we shall later become. My dear, I seem to have changed so little. The odor of rain through an open window, the poplar woods in the fog, a piece of music by Cimarosa that old ladies asked me to play because, I suppose, it brought back their youth, or even a special quality of silence that I find only at Woroïno, are enough to cancel out all the thoughts, events, and sorrows which lie between me and that childhood. I could almost claim that the intervening time has lasted less than an hour, that it has been only one of those moments of half-sleep into which I so often fell then, during which neither life nor I had time to change ourselves very much. I have only to close my eyes: everything happens exactly as it did then; I find again, as if he had never left me, the timid, sweet young boy who did not believe in complaining and who resembles me so much that I suspect, perhaps unjustly, that he resembled me completely.

I see that I am contradicting myself. Doubtless, all this is like those forebodings that one assumes one has had because one ought to have had them. The cruelest result of what I am obliged to call (if only to conform to common usage) our faults is when they contaminate even the memory of a time when we had not yet committed them. That is precisely what troubles me. For if I should be wrong, I cannot tell in what sense; and I shall never be able to determine if my innocence then was less than I am persuaded it was, or if I am now less guilty than I cause myself to think. But I see I have not managed to explain anything yet.

I need hardly tell you that we were very poor. There is something sad about the financial constraints of old families, where one seems to go on living only out of fidelity. You will ask, fidelity to what? To the house, I suppose, to the ancestors also, and simply to what one was. Oh, poverty does not have much importance for a child; nor had it for my mother and my sisters, since everyone knew us and no one thought us richer than we were. That was the advantage of those closed milieux back then, that one thought less about who you were than about who you had been. The past, however little one thinks about it, is something infinitely more stable than the present, and thus it seems to have a greater importance. No one paid more attention to us than was necessary. What they esteemed in us was a certain field marshal who had lived so long ago that no one remembered his dates or even the century in which he lived. I am also aware that the fortune of my grandfather and the distinctions achieved by my great-grandfather were things of great importance for us, more real than our own existence. These old-fashioned ways of looking at things will probably make you smile. I realize that other ways, completely opposite, would be no more unreasonable; but these were the ones that helped us live. Just as nothing could prevent us from being the descendants of these figures who had become almost legendary, so nothing could prevent people from continuing to honor them in us; it was, indeed, the only part of our patrimony that was truly inalienable. We were not looked down upon because we had less money or credit than they had had; that was only natural. But to have wished to equal these celebrated men would have been as unseemly as misplaced ambition.

Thus, the carriage that took us to church would have been deemed old-fashioned anywhere but at Woroïno, but there I think a new carriage would have been much more shocking; and if my mother's dresses lasted a little too long, no one paid any attention to that either. We Géras were simply the last of our line in this very ancient land of northern Bohemia. One might have thought that we no longer existed, that invisible men of eminence, much more imposing than we, continued to fill with their images the mirrors of our house. I want to avoid any impression of straining after an effect, especially at the end of a paragraph. But one might say that in a certain sense it is the living members of old families who seem to be the ghosts of the dead.

You must forgive me for lingering so long over

that Woroïno of olden times, but I loved it very much. That is a weakness of mine, no doubt, for I suppose one should not attach oneself so much to anything, at least not to anything in particular. It is not that we were terribly happy; at least, joy scarcely existed there. I do not remember ever having heard laughter, even the laughter of a young girl, which was not suppressed. One does not laugh much in old families. In the end, one gets used to speaking only in a low voice, as if afraid of awakening memories that are really better left to sleep in peace. But we were not unhappy either, and I should also admit that I never saw tears there. It is just that we were always a bit sad. That came more from character than from circumstance, and everyone around me agreed that it was possible to be happy without ceasing to be sad.

At that time it was the same white structure, all colonnades and windows, built in the French taste which had prevailed in the century of Catherine the Great. But you must remember that the old house was much more dilapidated then than it is today, since it was only repaired thanks to you during the years of our marriage. Yet it should not be hard for you to imagine it as it was then: just remember how it was when you came there the first time. Certainly it had not been erected for a life of monotony; I suppose it had been built to satisfy the fantasy of some ancestor who wanted to show off, and for giving fêtes there (in the time when one still gave fêtes). All the houses of the eighteenth century are like that. They seem to have been constructed for receiving guests, and as a result we never feel more than uneasy visitors in them. The house was not very comfortable for us: it was always too big and perpetually cold. It also seemed to me that it lacked solidity; and, indeed, the whiteness of similar houses, so desolate in the snow, suggests fragility. One recognizes that they were conceived for much warmer lands, by people who take life easily. But I now know that this architecture, in appearance so light that one would assume it was meant to last merely for a summer, will endure infinitely longer than we shall, and perhaps longer than our family. Possibly it will one day belong to strangers; that will not matter to it, for houses have their own private life in which our lives matter little and which we do not understand.

In my mind's eye I see the serious, slightly drawn faces there, the pensive faces of women in sitting rooms with white stucco walls. The ancestor I just spoke of had wanted the rooms spacious enough so that music would sound better there. He loved music. No one spoke of him very often; it seemed that they preferred not to mention him. He was known for having dissipated a large fortune. Perhaps they disliked him for that—or perhaps there was something else. The two subsequent generations were also passed over in silence, probably because there was nothing sufficiently remarkable in them to interest anyone. Then came my grandfather. He was ruined at the time of the agrarian reforms; he was a liberal; his ideas may well have been very good, but naturally they had impoverished him. My father's administration was equally deplorable. He died young, my father. I remember very little about him. I remember that he was severe with us children, as people often are who reproach themselves for not having known how to be severe with themselves. Of course, that is only an assumption—I really know nothing of my father.

There is one thing I have observed, Monique: people say that old houses always contain ghosts. I never saw any, and yet I was an easily frightened child. Perhaps I understood already that ghosts are invisible because we carry them within us. But what makes old houses disquieting is not that they have ghosts but that they might have them.

It is my belief that these years of infancy determined my life. I have other memories, more recent, more varied, possibly a good deal clearer, but it seems as if these closer impressions, although less monotonous, have not had the time to penetrate deeply enough into me. We are all distracted, because we have dreams; yet the perpetual repetition of the same things ends by impregnating us with them. My infancy was silent and solitary; it left me shy and consequently taciturn. When I think that I have known you for more than three years and that it is only now I dare speak to you for the first time! And even now it is only by letter, and only because I must. It is awful that silence can be such a fault; it is the worst of my faults, but I have committed it. Long before I committed it against you, I committed it against myself. Once silence has established itself in a house, it is hard to get it out; the more important a matter is, the more it seems one wants to keep it silent. It is almost like something frozen, increasingly hard and massive: life goes on under it, but imperceptibly. Woroïno was full of a silence which seemed ever bigger and bigger, and every silence is composed of nothing but unspoken words. Perhaps that is why I became a musician. Someone had to express this silence, make it render up all the sadness it contained, make it sing, as it were. Someone had to use not words, which are always too precise not to be cruel, but simply music; for music is never indiscreet, and when it laments, it does not explain why. Music of a particular kind was needed—slow, full of prolonged reticences, yet truthful, clinging to silence and finally drifting off into it. My music was of such a kind. You will clearly perceive that I am but an executant; I limit myself to interpretation. Yet one interprets only one's own trouble: for it is always of oneself that one speaks.

In the corridor that led to my room, there was a modern engraving no one ever looked at. It consequently belonged to me alone. I do not know who had put it there: since then I have so often seen it in the homes of people who call themselves artists that I have grown disgusted with it; but at that time I looked at it often. It depicted people listening to a musician, and I was almost terrified by the faces of these people to whom music seemed a revelation. I must have been thirteen then: neither music nor life, I assure you, had revealed anything to me yet. At least so I thought. But art causes the passions to speak such a beautiful language that more experience than I possessed was needed to comprehend what they wanted to say. I have since reread the little compositions in which I was experimenting with what I could achieve in those days: they are acceptable but much more infantile than my thoughts were. Yet that is always the case: our works represent a period of our existence we have already gone beyond at the time we write them. At that period, music put me in a state of torpor which was wholly agreeable but somewhat odd: everything seemed to be stopped except the beating of the arteries. The life seemed to have drained out of my body, and it seemed good to be so fatigued. It was a pleasure; it was virtually a kind of suffering as well. All my life I have found that pleasure and suffering are two very close sensations, and I think that is true for every reflective person. I remember also a very special sensitivity to touch—I mean the most innocent touch, the touch of a very soft material, the tickle of a fur which seemed a living pelt, or of the skin of a fruit. There is nothing blamable in that; such sensations were too ordinary for me to be much surprised by them: one is scarcely interested in what seems simple. Because they were not children, I gave the people in my engraving profound emotions. I imagined them as actors in a drama; I thought it undeniable that some drama had taken place. We are all the same: we fear drama; sometimes we are romantic enough to hope that there will be one, not recognizing that it has already commenced. There was also a picture in which one saw a man at the harpsichord who had suspended his playing in order to listen to his life. It was a very old copy of an Italian painting; the original is famous, but I do not know what it is called. You know how ignorant I am. I do not much like Italian paintings; and yet I loved that one. But I am not here to speak to you about a picture.

It was probably worth nothing. It was sold when money was scarce, with some antique furniture and some of those old enameled music boxes which know only one tune and always are missing the same note. Some of them contained marionettes. You wound them up; they made turns to the right and then several turns to the left; then they stopped. It was very touching. But I am not here to speak to you about marionettes.

I admit, Monique, that these pages contain too

much self-indulgence. But I have so few memories that are not bitter that you must pardon me if I pause over those which are merely sad. You will not be dismayed if I recount at length the thoughts of a child I alone know. You love children. I admit it: perhaps, without knowing, I have hoped in this way to enlist your indulgence at the beginning of an account which will ask much of you. I am also trying to gain time: that is only natural. Yet there is something absurd in shrouding with phrases a confession that should be simple: I would laugh at that, if only I could laugh. It is humiliating to think that so many chaotic hopes, emotions, and troubles (not counting all the suffering) have a physiological reason. That thought first made me ashamed before it calmed me. So life itself is nothing more than a physiological mystery. I do not see why pleasure should be held in contempt for being only a feeling, when no one holds grief in contempt and that, too, is a feeling. One respects grief because it is not voluntary; but it is a question whether pleasure is always voluntary or whether it is not inflicted on us. Even if it were otherwise, the pleasure freely chosen would not seem to me more sinful for that. But this is hardly the place to raise all these questions.

I realize that I am becoming very obscure. Certainly, one or two precise terms would suffice for me to explain myself, terms which are not even indecent, because they are scientific. But I shall not use them. Do not think that I fear them: one can hardly fear the words when one has consented to the deeds. Quite simply, I cannot use them. I cannot, not merely out of delicacy and because I am addressing you; I cannot use them even to myself. I know that there are names for every malady and that what I am speaking to you about is thought to be a malady. I myself thought so for a long time. But I am not a doctor, nor am I even sure that I am a sick man. Life, Monique, is far more complex than any of its possible definitions; every simplified image of life always risks being crude. But I also do not want you to suppose that I approve of poets who avoid exact terms because they know only their dreams; there is a good deal of truth in the dreams of poets, but they are not the whole of life. Life is something more than poetry. It is something more than physiology and more even than ethics, in which I believed for such a long time. It is all that and much more: it is life. It is our sole good and our sole curse. We live, Monique. Each of us has his own, unique life, determined by all the past about which we can do nothing, and which in turn determines, however little, all the future. His life. His life which belongs only to him, which will not take place a second time, and which he is not always sure he completely understands. And what I say about the whole of life, I could say about each moment of life. Other people see our presence, our gestures, the way words form on our lips;

only we see our life. How strange that is: we see it, we are amazed that it is as it is, and we cannot change it. Even when we sit in judgment on it, we belong to it all the more. Our approval or our disapproval is a part of it. Life always mirrors itself. Because there is nothing else: the world, for each of us, exists only insofar as it exists within the confines of our own life. And the elements of which it is composed are not separable: I know only too well that the instincts we are proud of and those we dare not admit have, ultimately, the same origin. We could not suppress one of them without changing all the others. Words serve so many people, Monique, that they are no longer useful to anyone. How can a scientific term explain a life? It does not even explain a deed; it simply designates it. It designates it in a manner always the same, and yet there are not two identical deeds in different lives, nor perhaps in the same life. Deeds are, after all, very simple. It is easy to account for them: perhaps you knew that already. But even when you know everything, I shall still have to explain myself.

This letter is an explanation. I do not wish it to become an apology. I am not foolish enough to hope that I shall be approved of; I do not even ask to be accepted: that is too great a demand. I wish only to be understood. I realize that is the same thing, and that it is to wish a great deal. But you have given me so much in small matters that I feel almost entitled to expect your comprehension in large ones.

I do not want you to imagine me more solitary than I was. I sometimes had companions, companions, that is, as young as I. It was generally at the time of the big holidays, when many people came to visit. Children came also, whom I often did not know. Or else it was on birthdays, when we went to visit distant relatives who seemed actually to exist only one day a year, since that was the only day we thought about them. Almost all the children were shy like me; as a result, we did not much enjoy each other. There were the impudent ones, so wild that one hoped they would go away, and others, no less wild, who tormented me without my protesting, because they were beautiful or had beautiful voices. I told you I was a child who was very sensitive to beauty. I foresaw already that beauty and the pleasure it brings us are worth every sacrifice and even worth every humiliation. I was by nature humble. I suppose I let myself be tyrannized by delights. It did not bother me that I was less handsome than my friends; I was happy to see them, and could not imagine it otherwise. It made me happy to love them; it never occurred to me to hope that they might love me. Love (forgive me, my dear) is a sentiment I have not felt since then; it requires too many virtues for me to be capable of it. I was amazed that my childhood could have had faith in a passion so vain, almost always mendacious, and not at all necessary, not even for sensual pleasure. But love, among children, is a part of candor. They imagine they love because they do not perceive that they desire. Such friendships were not frequent; the occasions hardly lent themselves; and for that reason they remained very innocent. My friends went away again, or else it was we who returned to our own house; once more, the solitary life would close about me. It occurred to me to write them letters, but I was so incapable of avoiding grammatical errors that I did not send them. In any case, I had nothing to say. Jealousy is a reprehensible sentiment, but one must pardon children for giving into it when so many rational adults are its victims. I suffered from it a great deal, all the more so as I did not admit it. I understood, of course, that friendship should never make one jealous; I already began to suspect I was sinful. But what I am telling you about is surely natural for boys: all children have known similar passions, and one would be wrong, wouldn't one, to suspect a grave danger there?

I was raised by women. I was the last son in a very numerous family; I had a sickly nature; my mother and my sisters were not very happy. So there were plenty of reasons why I was loved. There is so much goodness in the tenderness of women that for a long time now I have wanted to thank God for it. Our life, so austere, was quite frigid on the surface; we were afraid of my father, later of my older brothers; and nothing brings people together like being afraid together. Neither my mother nor my sisters were very expansive. Their presence was like dimmed lamps, which are very gentle and shed hardly any light but whose consistent glow prevents it from becoming too dark and prevents one from being truly alone. You cannot imagine how reassuring the calm affection of women was for an apprehensive child like myself. Their silence, their unimportant words which reflected nothing more than their calm, their familiar gestures which seemed to control things, their blank but tranquil faces which, somehow, resembled mine, taught me veneration. My mother died fairly early: you never knew her. Life and death also took away my sisters; but most of them were then so young that they seemed beautiful. All of them, I think, already possessed love, which they carried in the depths of themselves, in the same way that, later, when they had been married, they carried their infant or the illness of which they were to die. Nothing is so touching as those dreams of young girls, where so many dormant instincts are dimly expressed; theirs is an affecting beauty, for they give of themselves heedlessly, and ordinary life will not enjoy the use of them. I should explain that many of these love affairs were still very vague; they had for their objects the young men of the neighborhood, who were unaware of it. My sisters were very reserved; they rarely confided in one another. Sometimes they were ignorant of what they themselves felt. Naturally, I was much too young for them to confide in me; but I guessed what they were feeling and shared in their sorrows. When the man they were in love with would arrive unexpectedly, my heart raced, possibly more than theirs. It is dangerous, I am sure, for a sensitive adolescent to learn to view love through the dreams of young girls, even when they seem to be pure and he imagines himself to be pure also.

Once again, I find myself on the verge of a confession; it would be better to make it quickly and simply. To be sure, my sisters also had girlfriends who lived with us almost like members of the family and of whom I came to think myself the younger brother. Nothing would appear to have prevented me from loving one of these girls, and perhaps you yourself find it strange that I did not. Yet the fact is, it was impossible. An intimacy so familial, so peaceful, took away the curiosities and inquietudes of desire, even supposing I had been capable of them. I don't think the word "veneration," which I used a little while ago, is excessive when it is applied to a very good woman: I less and less believe it is excessive. I already had a suspicion (I even exaggerated it to myself) of how brutal the physical acts of love can be. It would have repelled me to join these images of domestic, rational, perfectly austere and pure life with other more passionate ones. One does not lose one's heart to what one respects, nor perhaps even to what one loves; above all, one does not lose one's heart to what resembles oneself—and it was not women I was most different from. You have the merit, my dear, not only of being able to understand everything but of being able to understand everything before it has been said. Monique, do you understand me?

I do not know when I myself first understood. Certain details, which I really cannot give you, indicate to me it must go very far back, even to the first memories of being, and that dreams are often the harbingers of desire. But an instinct is not yet a temptation; it simply makes temptation possible. Just now I appeared to explain my penchants by external influences. They certainly contributed to establishing them; yet I see clearly that one should always go back to much more intimate explanations, much more obscure ones, which we understand imperfectly because they are hidden within us. Having such instincts is not enough to explain the cause, and no one, after all, can explain that completely; therefore, I shall not insist. I would simply claim that these instincts, precisely because they were natural to me, were able to develop for a long time without my being aware of it. People who speak from hearsay are almost always wrong, because they look on from the outside and they perceive crudely. And they never imagine that the acts they judge reprehensible can be at once easy and spontaneous, as in fact most human acts are. They inveigh against the example set, the moral contagion, and they draw back only from the difficulty of explaining. They do not realize that nature is more diverse than we imagine; they do not wish to know that, because it is easier for them to be indignant than to think. They praise purity. They do not know how much anxiety purity can contain; they are, above all, unaware of the frankness of need. Between my fourteenth and sixteenth year, I had fewer young friends than formerly, because I was exceedingly withdrawn. Nevertheless, as I realize today, I was once or twice almost happy in complete innocence. I shall not explain what circumstances prevented me: that is too delicate a matter, and I have too much to say to linger over circumstances.

Books might have instructed me. I have often heard people bewail their influence; it would be easy to pretend I was their victim: that would perhaps make me more interesting. But books had no effect whatsoever on me. I have never loved books. Every time one opens them one expects some surprising revelation. But every time one closes them one feels a bit more discouraged. In any case, one would have to read everything, and a lifetime would not be enough for that. But books do not contain life; they contain only its ashes—and those ashes are, I suppose, what is called human experience. At home we had a good number of old volumes in a room no one ever went into. They were mostly collections of pious works, printed in Germany, full of that gentle Moravian mysticism that my ancestors liked. I was fond of that sort of book. The loves they depict have all the swooning and transport others do, but they do not contain the remorse. They can give themselves over to it fearlessly. There were also some quite different works (usually in French and written in the eighteenth century) which one does not put into the hands of children. But they did not please me either. Sensual pleasure, I already suspected, is a very grave subject: one should deal seriously with what can cause suffering. I remember certain pages which should have gratified my instincts, or rather awakened them, but which I turned with indifference because the images they offered me were far too precise. Things in life are never precise; and it is a lie to depict them nakedly, since we never see them except through a fog of desire. It is not true that books tempt us, nor do events, since they only tempt us when we are ready to be tempted and at a time when everything can tempt us. It is simply not true that a few coarse details can teach one about love; it is simply not true that it is easy to recognize, in the simple description of an act, the emotions that it will later produce in us.

Suffering is one. We speak of suffering as we speak of pleasure, but we speak of them when they do not possess us, when they no longer possess us. Each time they enter into us they create the surprise of a new feeling, and we are obliged to acknowledge that we had forgotten them. They are new, because we are. We bring to them each time a soul and a body slightly modified by life. And yet suffering is always the same. We know only several forms of it, as we do of pleasure, always the same ones, and we are their prisoners. Let me explain: our soul, I think, has only an abbreviated keyboard, and our life, whatever it does, cannot manage more than two or three poor notes. I remember the frightful dullness of certain evenings, when one clung to things as if to surrender to them—my musical excesses or my neurotic need of moral perfection, which was not perhaps anything more than a transposition of desire. I remember certain tears shed when, in truth, there was nothing to cry over. I recognize that all my experiences of grief were already contained within the first one. I have been able to suffer more, but I have not suffered differently; and in any case, each time one suffers one believes one is suffering more. But grief teaches us nothing about its cause. If I assumed anything, I would have assumed I had been infatuated by a woman. The only thing is, I could not imagine which one.

I was sent to the academy at Pressburg. My health was not very good; nervous ailments had manifested themselves; and all that had delayed my departure. But the education I received at home did not seem adequate, and it was thought that my taste for music was hindering my studies. It is true they were not brilliant. They were no better at school; I was a very mediocre student. My stay at the academy was in any case very brief. I spent little more than two years at Pressburg. Presently, I shall explain why. But do not imagine any exciting adventures: nothing took place, or at least nothing happened to me.

I was sixteen years old. I had always lived withdrawn into myself; the long months at Pressburg taught me life, that is to say, the life of other people. It was, accordingly, a very painful time. When I think back on it, I see a great gray wall, the bleak rows of beds, the morning bell in the chill dawn when the flesh feels miserable and existence orderly, dull, and disheartening, like food that one eats without interest. Most of my fellow students belonged to the world from which I had come, and I was acquainted with several of them. But communal life develops brutality. I was shocked by the brutality of their games, of their habits, of their language. Nothing is more cynical than the talk of adolescents, even and above all when it is chaste. Many of my fellow students lived in a sort of perpetual obsession with women, probably less reprehensible than I thought, but which found its expression in crude vulgarity. Sad creatures seen on outings infatuated the oldest of my companions, but they caused me an extreme revulsion. I had been accustomed to bestow on women all the standard concepts of respect. I hated them when they were not worthy of it. My strict education partly explains it, but I fear there was something more in this repulsion than a simple indication of innocence. I had the illusion of purity. I smile when I think how often it is like that: we believe we are pure insofar as we despise what we do not desire.

I have not blamed books; I blame even less examples. I believe, my dear, only in inner temptation. I do not for a moment deny that the examples overwhelmed me, but not in the way you might imagine. I was terrified. I do not say that I was outraged—that is too simple a feeling. I *believed* I was outraged. I was a scrupulous young boy, full of what are called the noblest sentiments. I attached an almost neurotic importance to physical purity, probably because, without knowing it, I also attached a great deal of importance to the body; indignation, therefore, seemed to me natural; and anyway, I needed a word to designate what I was feeling. I know now that it was really fear. I have always been afraid, with an undefined, ceaseless fear, a fear of something which I imagined might be monstrous and which would paralyze me in advance. From that time on, the object of this fear was precise. It was as if I had just discovered a contagious disease spreading around me and, even though I pretended the contrary, was fully aware that it could touch me. I knew, confusedly, that such things existed; no doubt I did not imagine them quite this way, or (since I must tell you everything) my instinct, at the time of my studies, was less aroused. Before, I had imagined these things as rather vague acts, which had taken place in some other time or which happened elsewhere, but which had no reality for me. Now I saw them everywhere. At night, in my bed, I suffocated thinking of them; I genuinely thought that I was suffocating from disgust. I did not know that disgust is one of the forms of obsession and that, if one longs for something, it is easier to think of it with horror than not to think of it at all. I thought of it continually. Most of those I suspected were probably not guilty, yet I came to suspect everyone. I was used to examining my conscience; I should have suspected myself. Naturally, I did nothing of the kind. It was impossible for me to imagine myself, without any actual proof, as having sunk to the level of my own disgust; and I continue to believe I was different from the others.

A moralist would not have seen any difference. And yet it seems to me that I was not like the others and even that I was worth rather more than they. First of all, because I had scruples, and because those I am telling you about certainly had none whatever. Then, because I loved beauty, because I loved it exclusively, and because it had restricted my choice, which was not their case at all. Finally, because I was more particular, or, if you will, more refined. It was precisely those refinements that deceived me. I took for virtue what is only squeamishness, and the one scene I witnessed by chance would surely have shocked me much less if the actors in it had been more attractive.

To the degree that communal existence became more distasteful to me, I suffered more and more from being emotionally alone. At least, I attributed my suffering to emotional causes. The simplest things irritated me; I thought myself suspect, as if I were already guilty; an idea I could not shake off poisoned all my relationships. I fell ill. It would be more accurate to say that I became increasingly ill; for I always was somewhat ill.

It was not a serious illness. It was *my* illness, which I was to know many more times and which I had known already. For each of us has his own illness, like his own hygiene and his own health, which it is difficult to diagnose with complete precision. It was a rather prolonged illness. It lasted several weeks; and, as always happens, it brought me a little calm. The images which had obsessed me during my fever went away with it; what remained was nothing more than a confusion of shame, similar to the bad taste that a bout of fever leaves behind, and the recollections of those images got all mixed up in my beclouded memory. Then, just as an obsessive thought will disappear for a moment only if another replaces it, I gradually saw my second obsession begin to grow. Death tempted me. It has always seemed to me fairly easy to die. My way of imagining death scarcely differed from my way of imagining love: I saw in it a failing, a defeat that would be sweet. From that time on, throughout my entire life, these two obsessions have never ceased to alternate within me; the one would heal me from the other, and no rational argument could heal me from both. I lay in my infirmary bed; I looked through the window at the gray wall of the neighboring courtyard as the raucous voices of children filled the air. I said to myself that life would forever be this gray wall, these raucous voices, and the distress of my hidden trouble. I told myself that nothing was worth it and that it was easy not to want to live any more. And slowly, as if it were some sort of answer I gave myself, music surged up within me. At first it was funereal music, but it soon ceased to be anything that fits that description; for death no longer makes any sense in a place life cannot reach, and this music floated high above both death and life. It was a peaceful music, peaceful because it was powerful. It filled the whole infirmary, swaying me like the rocking of a steady, slow groundswell, sensuously; I did not fight against it, and for an instant I felt calmed. I was no longer a sick young man frightened of himself: I felt myself become who I really was; for all of us would be transformed if we had the courage to be who we really are. Suddenly it seemed easy for me, who am too shy to seek or even endure applause, to become a great musician, to unveil to others this new music which pulsed within me like a heartbeat. One of the patients coughing in a far corner of the room interrupted this fantasy abruptly, and I realized that my pulse was, quite simply, racing too rapidly.

I recovered. I knew the emotions of convalescence and its tears trembling on the fringe of eyelids. My sensibility, sharpened by suffering, was even more repulsed by the abrasions of school. I suffered from a lack of solitude and from a lack of music. All my life, music and solitude have had a calming influence upon me. The interior struggles which had taken place within me without my being aware of them, and the illness which had followed them, had exhausted my strength. I was so weak that I became very pious. I acquired that facile spirituality which is produced by all great weaknesses. It permitted me to despise even more sincerely what I told you about just now and what I started thinking about again. I could no longer live in an atmosphere that had been soiled for me. I wrote absurd letters to my mother, exaggerated yet true, in which I begged her to take me out of school. I told her that I was unhappy there, that I wanted to become a great musician, but that I would cost her no more money, that I would quickly become self-sufficient. And yet, in fact, school had become less hateful than it had been. Many of my schoolmates, who at the beginning had tormented me, now showed greater kindness toward me; I was so easy to please that I felt a great gratitude to them; I thought that I had been wrong, that they had not been wicked. I shall always remember a young boy to whom I had barely spoken, who, when he realized I was quite poor and that my family sent me almost nothing, insisted on sharing his sweets with me. I had become absurdly sensitive, which humiliated me; I had such a need for affection that it caused me to burst into tears, and I remember being ashamed of those tears, as if they were a sort of sin. From that day, we were friends. In other circumstances, the beginning of such a friendship would have made me want to put off my departure, but here, on the contrary, it confirmed my desire to get out, and as soon as possible. I wrote even more pressing letters to my mother. I begged her to take me away without delay.

My mother was very good. She was always good to me. She came and got me herself. I should also explain that my tuition was expensive: each semester, it was a worry for my family. If my studies had been better, I doubt that they would have taken me out of school, but I did not do any work, and my brothers decided that it was money wasted. It seems to me they were not wholly wrong. The oldest had just got married; that had been an additional expense. When I got back to Woroïno, I saw that they had relegated me to a remote wing of the house, but naturally I did not complain. My mother insisted that I try to eat; she wanted to serve me herself; she smiled with that weak smile which seemed always to ask pardon that she could not do more than she did. Her fingers and her hands seemed to me as worn as her dress, and I observed that her fingers, whose delicacy I admired, were beginning to be spoiled by work, like those of a quite poor woman. I was aware that I had disappointed her, that she had hoped for me something other than a future as a musician, quite probably a mediocre musician at that. But, nonetheless, she was content to see me again. I did not tell her my schoolboy sorrows; by now they seemed to me completely imaginary compared to the difficulties and efforts that mere existence represented for my family; in any case, it was a difficult thing to talk about. I even came to feel a kind of respect for my brothers. They administered what was still called the domain; that was more than I did or ever would do; and I began vaguely to understand that that had its importance.

You will suppose that my return was sad; on the contrary, I was happy. I felt saved. You will perhaps guess that it was from myself that I felt saved. It was an absurd feeling, all the more so because I experienced it several times afterward, which proves that it was never definitive. My school years had been little more than an interlude; I really did not think much more about them. I was not yet disabused of my pretended perfection. I was content to live according to the ideal of the passive, rather dreary morality that I heard preached around me; and I thought this type of existence might last forever. I set myself seriously to work; I managed to fill my days with such continuous music that the moments of silence seemed nothing more than pauses. Music does not facilitate thought; it facilitates only dreams, and the most vague dreams at that. I seemed to fear whatever could distract me from these dreams, or perhaps whatever might define them in detail. I had not reestablished any of my childhood friendships: whenever my family went on a visit, I begged them to leave me behind. That was a reaction against the communal life imposed by school; it was also a precaution, but I took it without admitting that fact to myself. A number of vagabond gypsies went through our region; some are good musicians, and, as you know, their race is often very handsome. In earlier times, when I was much younger, I used to speak with their children through the garden fence, and, not knowing what to say, I gave them flowers. I wonder if the flowers gave them much pleasure. But, since my return, I had become more reasonable, and I went out only in broad daylight.

I did not have any secret thoughts; I thought as little as possible. I remember, with some irony, how pleased I was with myself that I had given myself completely to my studies. I was like someone who has a fever and does not find his torpor disagreeable yet fears to move, since the slightest movement can make him shiver. That was what I called calm. I have learned since that one must fear this calm in which one slumbers when one is on the edge of events. We believe we are tranquil, possibly because something, unbeknownst to us, has already been decided within us.

That was when it happened—on a morning like all the others, when nothing, neither my mind nor my body, gave me any clearer warning than usual. I do not claim that the circumstances took me by surprise: they were already there without my going out to meet them. But circumstances are like that. They are shy and indefatigable; they come and go before our doorway, always the same, and it is up to us whether we stretch out our hand to stop these passersby. It was a morning like every other morning, neither more radiant nor more overcast. I was walking in the country down a road lined with trees; everything was silent, as if listening to itself live; my thoughts, I assure you, were no less innocent than the day which was beginning. At least, I cannot recall thoughts that were not innocent; for as soon as they ceased to be innocent, I ceased to take account of them. At that moment when I seemed to distance myself from the force of nature, I am obliged to praise it for being everywhere present in the form of necessity. The fruit falls only in its own time, since its weight has long been pulling it toward the earth: this inner ripening is the only fatality. I can tell you about this only in a very vague way: I was walking;

I had no destination; it was not my fault if, on this particular morning, I encountered beauty . . .

I came home. I do not want to dramatize; you would quickly perceive I had exaggerated the truth. What I felt was not shame, even less remorse; it was, rather, stupor. I had never imagined so much simplicity in what had so terrified me in advance: the facility of sin discouraged repentence. The simplicity that pleasure taught me I was to rediscover much later in great poverty, in grief, in sickness, in death—I mean in the death of others, but I hope one day to rediscover it in my own death. It is our imagination which causes us to dress things up, but things themselves are divinely naked. I went home. My head was spinning a bit; I have never been able to remember how I passed the rest of the day; the quivering of my nerves took a long time to subside. I can only remember going back to my room in the evening, and then the absurd but utterly painless tears which were nothing more than a release. All my life I have confused desire and fear; I no longer felt either one or the other. I do not say that I was happy: I wasn't sufficiently accustomed to happiness; I was merely stunned to be so little overwhelmed.

Every happiness is an innocence. I must, even if I shock you, repeat this word which always seems so miserable, for nothing better demonstrates our misery than the importance of happiness. During several weeks, I lived with my eyes closed. I had not abandoned music; on the contrary, I felt its great capacity for moving me. You know that weightlessness one experiences in the depths of dreams. It seemed that the early morning moments liberated me from my body for the rest of the day. My impressions at that time, varied though they were, are all one in my memory. One would have said that my sensibility, no longer restricted to myself, had expanded out into everything. The emotions of the morning extended into the musical phrases of the evening. Certain nuances of the season, a certain odor, an old melody I was taken with then, have remained for me eternal temptresses, because they speak to me of another person. Then, one morning, he came no more. My fever subsided: it was as if I had awakened. I can only compare it to the wonder created by the silence when music has ceased.

I had to reflect on what had happened. Naturally, I could only judge myself according to the accepted ideas of my world. I would have found it even more abominable not to be horrified by my sin than to have committed it; hence, I condemned myself severely. What frightened me above all else was to have been able to live in this way, to have been happy for several weeks before I was struck with the idea of sin. I tried to recall the circumstances of the act; I could not manage to; they overwhelmed me far more than at the moment in which I was living them, because in those moments I was not watching myself live. I pretended I had given in to a passing folly; I failed to see that my examinations of conscience had rapidly led me into a much worse folly: for I was too scrupulous not to attempt to become the most unhappy person I could.

In my room, I had one of those little old-fashioned mirrors which are always a bit blurred, as if a breath had clouded the glass. Since such an important thing had taken place within me, I naïvely thought I ought to have changed. But the mirror gave back only my ordinary image, an uncertain, timorous, pensive face. I passed my hand over it, less to wipe away the trace of a touch than to assure myself that it was indeed I. What perhaps makes sensual pleasure so terrible is that it teaches us we have a body. Up to that point, it has served us only for living. Then we realize that this body has its own special existence, its own dreams, its own will, and that until our death we shall have to take account of it, give in to it, negotiate with it, or struggle against it. We feel (we believe we feel) that our soul is only its finest dream. Sometimes, alone, before a mirror which redoubled my anguish, it would occur to me to ask what I had in common with my body, with its pleasures or its ills, as if I did not belong to it. But I do belong to it, my dear. This body, which appears so fragile, is nonetheless more durable than my virtuous resolutions, perhaps even more durable than my soul, for often the soul dies in advance of the body. That phrase,

Monique, will no doubt shock you more than my entire confession; for you believe in the immortality of the soul. Forgive me if I am less sure than you, or if I have less pride; at times, the soul seems to me nothing more than a simple respiration of the body.

I believed in God. I had a very human conception of Him—that is to say, very inhuman—and I judged myself an abomination before Him. Life, which alone teaches us about life, explains to us also the books we have read. Certain passages of the Bible that I had read carelessly took on for me a new intensity; they panicked me. Sometimes I said to myself that it had happened, that nothing could have prevented its having happened, and that I could only resign myself to it. Such a thought was like that of damnation: it calmed me. There is a certain release at the bottom of all great helplessness. I promised myself only that it would never happen again; I swore it to God—as if God accepted oaths. My sin had as its only witness my accomplice, and he was no longer there. It is the opinion of others that gives our acts a sort of reality. Mine, unknown by anyone, had little more reality than the deeds done in a dream. I could have claimed, so much did my exhausted mind take refuge in lies, that nothing at all had taken place: it is, after all, no more ridiculous to deny the past than to pledge the future.

What I had experienced was not at all love, and even less a passion. Ignorant as I was, I recognized this. It was an involvement that I was able to believe was completely external to me. I placed all the responsibility for it on the person who had merely shared it; I persuaded myself that my separation from him had been voluntary and was meritorious. I knew very well that that was not true, but then, it might have been: we can dupe our memory also. As a result of repeating to ourselves what we should have done, we end up finding it impossible to believe that we have not done it. Vice for me consisted in the habit of sin; I did not know that it is more difficult to give in once than never to give in. Explaining away my fault as, in effect, the result of circumstances to which I vowed never to expose myself again, I in some way separated it from myself in order to see it as nothing more than an accident. My dear, I must confess everything to you: after having sworn never to repeat it, I regretted a little less having done it once.

I shall spare you the recital of new transgressions which destroyed my illusion that I had been only half guilty. You will reproach me for being so self-indulgent about my memories; perhaps you are right. I am now so far away from the adolescent that I was, from his ideas, from his sufferings, that I am drawn toward him with a sort of affection; I should like to feel sorry for him, and even to console him. This feeling, Monique, leads me to reflect: I wonder if it is not the memory of our own youth that seduces us in the presence of the youth of others. I was terrified at the facility with which I, so shy, so slow to comprehend, managed to foresee potential complicities; I was ashamed not so much of my faults as of the tawdry circumstances, as if it were up to me alone to choose less contemptible ones. I was deprived of the relief of feeling irresponsible: I knew very well that my acts were voluntary, but then I only willed them at the moment when I was actually achieving them. One would have said that instinct, in order to take hold of me, waited until my conscience had faded away or closed her eyes. One after another, I yielded to two contradictory impulses of will which did not clash with each other because they came one after the other. And yet sometimes an occasion offered itself that I did not seize: I was shy. In that way, my triumphs over myself constituted only another defeat; our defeats are sometimes the best adversaries we can pit against our vices.

I had no one of whom I could ask advice. The first consequence of forbidden inclinations is to wall us up within ourselves. One must keep silent or speak only to fellow accomplices. In my efforts to conquer myself, I suffered a good deal from not being able to hope for either encouragement or pity, or even for that bit of esteem that good will always merits. I had never been intimate with my brothers; my mother, who was pious and sad, had touching illusions about me; she would have hated to have me destroy the terribly pure, terribly sweet, somewhat mawkish idea she had conceived of her child. If I had dared confess to my family, what they would have been able to pardon least would have been precisely the confession itself. I would have placed these scrupulous people in an awkward situation, which ignorance spared them. I would have been scrutinized; I would not have been helped. In family life, our role is fixed once and for all by its relationship to the roles of others. One is the son, the brother, the husband, and so on. This role belongs to us like our name, the state of health we are thought to have, and the deference we are, or are not, supposed to be shown. The rest is of no importance; the rest is our life. Sometimes at the table, or in a tranquil drawing room, I had moments of agony when I thought I would die. I was surprised that no one perceived them. It seems at such times that the space stretching between us and the members of our family is uncrossable: one struggles in solitude as if at the center of a crystal. I came to believe that these people were wise enough to understand, not to intervene, and not to be surprised. Such a hypothesis, if one thinks about it, could perhaps explain God. But when it concerns ordinary mortals, it is useless to attribute wisdom to them: blindness is enough.

If you think about my family life as I have described it to you, you can understand how this environment was as dreary as an endless November. I imagined that a less sad existence would also be more pure; I thought as well, correctly, that nothing pushes us to the excesses of our instincts like the regularity of a life which is conventionally correct. We passed the winter at Pressburg. The health of one of my sisters necessitated our living in town because of the proximity of doctors. My mother, who did her best to contribute to my future, had insisted that I take harmony lessons; everyone said that I had made enormous progress. Certainly, I worked the way people work when they are seeking refuge in an occupation. The musician who taught me (he was a rather mediocre man, but full of good will) advised my mother to send me abroad to complete my musical education. I knew existence there would be hard; and yet I longed to go. We are attached by so many ties to the places where we have lived that it seems to us that, by leaving them, we can more easily leave ourselves.

My health, which had much improved, was no longer an obstacle; my mother, however, thought me too young. Perhaps she feared the temptations a freer life would expose me to. She imagined, I suppose, that life within the family had saved me from them. Many parents assume that. She understood that it was necessary for me to earn some money, but no doubt she thought that could wait. At that time I did not guess at the poignancy of her refusal. I was unaware that she did not have long to live.

One evening at Pressburg, shortly after the death of my sister, I returned home in greater disarray than usual. I had loved my sister a great deal. I do not pretend that her death afflicted me excessively; I was too tormented within myself to be terribly moved. Suffering turns us into egotists, for it absorbs us completely: it is later, in the form of memory, that it teaches us compassion. I came back a little earlier than I had intended; but I had not set a specific hour with my mother, and therefore she was not expecting me. As I opened the door, I found her sitting in the dark. In the last weeks of her life, my mother liked to sit and do nothing as night approached. It seemed almost as if she wished to accustom herself to immobility and darkness. I suppose her face took on then that calmer, more sincere expression we have when we are all alone and in complete darkness. I walked in. My mother did not like to be surprised in that way. She told me, as if to excuse herself, that the lamp had just gone out; but I put my hands on it; the glass was not even warm. She perceived clearly that something was wrong: when it is dark we are more clairvoyant because our eyes do not deceive us. Feeling my way, I took a seat near her. I was in a rather curious state of languor which I knew only too well. It felt as though a confession was going to pour out of me, involuntarily, like tears. I was doubtless on the verge of recounting everything, when the maid entered with another lamp.

Then I realized that I could say nothing more, that I would not be able to tolerate the expression my mother's face would assume once she had understood me. This little bit of light spared me an irreparable, pointless error. Confidences, my dear, are always pernicious when their goal is not to simplify the life of another person.

I had gone too far to maintain silence; I was obliged to speak. I described the sadness of my existence, my vague, remote chances for the future, the subservience in which my brothers held me within the family. I was thinking of a much worse subservience from which I hoped to deliver myself by leaving. I invested these shabby complaints with all the distress I would have put into another confession, which I could not make and which was the only thing that mattered to me. My mother kept silent; I realized that I had persuaded her. She rose to go to the door. She was weak and tired; I recognized how painful it had been for her that she had been unable to say no to me. It was as if she had lost a second child. It pained me not to be able to tell her the real cause of my importunity; she must have thought me very egotistical; I wish I could have told her I would not go. The next day she called me to her; we spoke about my departure as if it had always been agreed between us. My family was not rich enough to give me an allowance: I would have to work to live. In order to help me get started, my mother gave me, in strictest secrecy, some money taken from her own funds. It was not a large sum, yet it seemed so to both of us. I reimbursed her in part as soon as I was able; but my mother died too soon, and I was not able to discharge my debt altogether. My mother believed in my future. If I have ever desired any glory or fame, it is because I knew it would make her happy. Thus, insofar as those we have loved disappear, the reasons diminish for achieving a happiness that we can no longer share together.

I was about to be nineteen. It mattered to my mother that I should not leave until after my birthday; we therefore returned to Woroïno. During the few weeks I spent there, I had no deed to reproach myself with, and almost no desire. I was simply occupied with the preparations for my departure.

I wanted to go before the Easter season, which brings too many strangers into the region. On the last evening, I said goodbye to my mother. We separated without any ado. There is something reprehensible about acting too emotionally when one goes away, as if one wanted to make oneself missed. Then, too, sensuous kisses cause us to forget the other kind: one no longer knows how to give the other kind, or one no longer dares. I wanted to leave the next morning very early without disturbing anyone. I spent the night in my room in front of my open window, trying to imagine my future. It was an immense and bright night. The park was separated from the main road only by a fence; some people returning late passed down the road in silence; I heard their heavy footsteps grow distant. Suddenly a sad song floated up from them. It is possible that these poor people thought and suffered only dimly, like inanimate objects. But their song contained whatever soul they were capable of. They sang merely to lighten their road; they were unaware of what they were expressing. I recall the voice of the woman, so limpid it could have flown indefatigably, indefinitely up to God. I thought it not impossible that the whole of life itself might become a similar ascension; I solemnly promised that to myself. It is not hard to cultivate admirable thoughts when the stars are out. It is much harder to keep them intact in the paltriness of the day. It is so much harder to be to others what we are to God.

I arrived in Vienna. My mother had inculcated me with all the Moravian prejudices against Austria; the first week I spent there was so painful that I would prefer to say nothing about it. I took a room in a rather poor house. I was full of good intentions; I remember that I believed I could methodically arrange my desires and anguishes, the way one arranges objects in a drawer. There is, in the renunciations of a twenty-year-old, a bitter intoxication. I had read, I forget in which book, that at a specific time of adolescence certain troubles are not rare; I antedated my memories to prove to myself that there had been merely some very banal incidents limited to a period of life I had gone beyond. I did not even dream of other forms of happiness; I therefore had to choose between my penchants, which I judged criminal, and complete renunciation, which is perhaps not human. I chose. I condemned myself, at the age of twenty, to an absolute isolation of the senses and the heart. Thus began a number of years of struggle, obsession, and severity. I cannot say that my efforts were admirable; one can only say that they were senseless. In any case, it is something to have made them; they allow me today to accept myself more honorably. Precisely because I would have been able to find, in this unknown town, easier opportunities, I felt obliged to repulse them all; I did not wish to betray the confidence which had been shown me in allowing me to leave home. Yet it is strange to see how quickly we become habituated to ourselves; I found it admirable to renounce what, several months earlier, I believed I was horrified by.

I have told you how I had found a room in a pretty miserable house. Good Lord, I had no aspirations for anything better. But what makes poverty so hard is not its deprivations but its promiscuity. Our situation at Pressburg had shielded me from the sordid contacts one experiences in cities. Despite the recommendations my family had furnished me with, for a long time it was difficult, at my age, to find a job giving lessons. I did not like to thrust myself forward, and therefore I did not know how to go about it. It pained me to serve as an accompanist in the theater, where the people around me thought they were putting me at ease by being excessively familiar. Nor did I form there the best opinion of women, whom one is supposed to be able to love. Unhappily, I was very sensitive to the external aspects of things; I suffered from living where I did; I suffered from the people I was sometimes obliged to encounter there. You can imagine how mediocre they were. But I have always been helped in my relations with people by the realization that they are not very happy. Objects are not very happy either; that is what makes us feel friendly toward them. At first, my room revolted me; it was sad, with a sort of false elegance that wrung the heart because it revealed that the owner of the house did not know any better. It was not very clean either: it was evident that other people had been there before me, and that disgusted me a good deal. Later I came to get interested in who they might have been and in imagining their life. They were like friends with whom I could not get involved because I did not know them. I told myself that they had sat at this table to labor over their daily accounts, that they had known on this bed their sleep or their insomnia. I thought how they had had their hopes, their virtues, their vices, and their miseries, as I had my own. I do not know, my dear, what the point of suffering is if it does not teach us pity.

I got accustomed to it all. One gets accustomed easily. There is a sort of enjoyment in knowing that one is poor, that one is alone, and that no one is thinking of you. It simplifies life. But it is also a great temptation. I came back late every night through quarters almost deserted at that hour, so tired that I no longer felt fatigue. The people you encounter in the streets during the day give the impression of going toward a definite goal, which one assumes is rational; but at night they seem to walk in their dreams. The people who passed me seemed, like me, to have the vague aspect of figures one sees in dreams, and I was not convinced that the whole of life was not a stupid, exhausting, endless nightmare. I do not need to tell you the dullness of those Viennese nights. Sometimes I saw lovers reclining on doorsteps, insouciantly extending their conversations or perhaps their embraces; the darkness around them made the reciprocal illusion of love more excusable; and I envied this calm contentment that I did not desire. My dear, we are indeed strange. I experienced for the first time the perverse pleasure of being different from others. It is hard not to consider oneself superior when one suffers more. And the vision of happy people makes one feel a nausea at that sort of bliss.

I feared to find myself back in my room, to stretch out on that bed where I was sure not to be able to sleep. And yet I was obliged to return there. Even when I did not return until dawn, having broken my promises to myself (I assure you, Monique, that happened only rarely), I was obliged in the end to climb up to my room, take off once again my clothing as I would perhaps have wished to be able to take off my body, and lie down between the sheets, where, this time, sleep came. Pleasure is too ephemeral; music lifts us up for a moment only to leave us sadder; but sleep is a compensation. Even when it leaves us, we take several seconds to begin suffering again; and each time one falls asleep, one has the sensation of surrendering to a friend. I am well aware that it is a faithless friend, like all the others; when we are too unhappy, it, too, abandons us. But we know that it will come back sooner or later, perhaps under another name, and that in the end we shall take repose in it. It is perfect when it is dreamless; one could say that, every night, it awakens us from life.

I was absolutely alone. Up to now I have kept silent about the human faces in which my desire was incarnated; I have interposed between you and me only anonymous phantoms. Do not think shame constrains me, or that jealousy one feels even with regard to one's memories. I do not flatter myself that I loved. I have experienced too often how short-lived the strongest emotions are to wish to draw from the coming together of perishable beings, hedged on every side by death, a sentiment that claims to be deathless. What moves us in another person has, after all, only been lent to him by life. I know too well that the soul grows old like the flesh, is, even in the best of us, only the flourishing of a season, an ephemeral miracle like youth itself. What is the point, my dear, of relying on what is transient?

I feared the bonds of habit derived from factitious pity, sensual deception, and lazy familiarity. It seems to me that I could only have loved a perfect being; I would be too mediocre for such a being to accept me even if he could one day be found. That is not all, my dear. Our soul, our mind, and our body have exigencies that are generally contradictory; I think it is difficult to combine such diverse satisfactions without debasing some and discouraging others. Therefore, I have put love aside. I do not wish to dignify my acts with metaphysical explanations when my shyness is a sufficient cause. I have almost always limited myself to trite encounters, through a vague fear of becoming attached and then suffering. It is enough to be the prisoner of an instinct without also being the prisoner of a passion; and I sincerely believe that I have never really been in love.

And then memories sweep over me. Do not be afraid: I shall not describe any of them; I shall not even tell you the names; I have even forgotten the names, or never actually knew them. I can see the particular curve of a neck, or a mouth or a cheek, certain faces loved for their sadness, the curb of weariness which pulled down their lips, or even that indefinable ingenuousness which is part of the perversity of an ignorant, laughing youth: everything that brings the soul to the surface of a body. I think of unknown persons I shall never see again, whom I do not particularly wish to see again, and whom, precisely because of that, I can speak of or be silent about with sincerity. I did not love them. I did not wish to hold on to the little happiness they brought me; I did not hope for understanding from them, or even for a lasting tenderness: quite simply, I listened to their life. Life is the mystery of every being: it is so admirable that one can always love it. Passion has need of cries, love itself takes pleasure in words, but sympathy can be silent. I have felt it, not only in anticipated moments of gratitude and satisfaction, but also toward people from whom I had no thought of any joy whatsoever. I have known it in silence, when those who inspired such sympathy would not have understood it. It is not necessary for someone to understand it. In the same way I have loved the characters of my dreams, poor, mediocre people, and sometimes women. But women, however much they may claim the opposite, always see tenderness as leading to love.

In the room next door to mine lived a young girl named Marie. Do not imagine that Marie was very beautiful; she had a quite ordinary face one would pass without noticing. Marie was little better than a servant. She had a job, but I doubt if her work would have provided her with enough to live on. In any case, whenever I visited her I always found her alone. I suppose she arranged it so that she would be alone at those times.

Marie was not intelligent, nor perhaps terribly good, but she was obliging in the way the poor are, who understand the necessity of mutual help. Friendship seems to take for them the form of quotidian small change. One should be grateful for the smallest token of kindness, and that is why I speak of Marie. She had authority over no one; she liked, I think, to have it over me. She advised me how to dress warmly or how to light my fire, and she busied herself by doing a lot of useful little things in my room. I cannot really say that Marie reminded me of my sisters, and yet I found in her all those sweet feminine movements I had loved as a child. One could see that she was trying hard to have good manners, and that in itself is laudable. Marie thought she loved music; she truly did love it: unhappily, she had execrable taste. It was a bad taste that was almost touching in its innocence. The most stereotyped sentiments seemed to her the most beautiful. One might say that her soul was content, as she herself was, with cheap imitation jewelry. Marie was capable of lying with the utmost sincerity. I suppose she lived, like most women, in some imaginary existence where she was better and happier than in real life. For example, if I had asked her, she would have sworn that she had never had lovers; she would have wept if I had not believed her. In the depths of herself she kept the memory of a childhood spent in the country, in the most virtuous circumstances, and also the memory of some vague fiancé. She also had other memories she did not speak of. The memory of women is like those old-fashioned sewing tables they have. There are secret drawers; there are others, shut so long that they cannot be opened. There are dried flowers in them which have become nothing more than the dust of roses, some entangled skeins, here and there some pins. Marie's memory was very serviceable: she used it to embroider her past.

I visited her in the evening once the cold weather began and I was afraid to remain alone. Our conversation was certainly dull, but there is something soothing for those who secretly torment themselves in listening to a woman speak about unimportant things. Marie was lazy; it did not surprise her that I worked so little. I have nothing of the fairy-tale prince about me. I was unaware that women, especially when they are poor, often think they have met the hero of their dreams even when the resemblance is hopelessly remote. My situation, and possibly my name, had for Marie a storybook prestige that I did not realize. To be sure, I was always extremely reserved toward her; she was flattered by that at the beginning, as by a sort of refinement she was not accustomed to. I did not guess what she was thinking as she sewed in silence; I merely thought that she liked me; and then, too, certain ideas simply did not occur to me.

Little by little I became aware that Marie was acting much more coolly. There was a sort of aggressive deference in her slightest words, as if she had suddenly realized that I came from a world much superior to her own. I felt she was angry. It did not surprise me that Marie's affection had passed: everything passes. I merely saw that she was sad; I was naïve enough not to guess why. I thought it impossible that she should suspect a certain aspect of my existence; it did not occur to me that she would probably have been less scandalized by it than I was. In the end, other circumstances supervened; I was obliged to move to a humbler house, my room having become too expensive for me. I never saw Marie again. How difficult it is, whatever precautions one takes, not to cause suffering.

I continued to struggle. If virtue consists in a series of efforts, I was irreproachable. I learned the danger of too hasty self-denials; I ceased to believe that perfection lay on the other side of a vow. Wisdom, like life itself, appeared to me to be comprised of continuing progress, of starting over again, of patience. A gradual recovery seemed to me less precarious: like the poor, I was content with miserable small gains. I tried to space out the crises. I indulged in a maniacal calculation of months, weeks, and days. Without admitting it to myself, during these periods of excessive discipline I survived only by looking ahead to the moment when I would allow myself to give in again. I ended by giving in to the first temptation that came along, simply because, for too long, I had forbidden myself to do so. I plotted in advance the timetable for my next weakness; I always gave myself over to it a little too hastily, less out of impatience for this pitiful happiness than to avoid the horror of waiting for its arrival and of enduring it. I shall spare you the recital of the precautions I took against myself; they now seem to me more demeaning than my faults. At first I thought it was important to avoid the opportunities for sin; I soon recognized that our actions have only the significance of symptoms: it is our nature we have to change. I was afraid of what might happen; I was afraid of my body; I ended by recognizing that our instincts communicate themselves to our soul and penetrate us completely. At that point there was no longer any refuge for me. In even the most innocent thoughts I discovered the beginnings of temptation. I did not find a single one that remained healthy for long; they seemed to go bad within me; and my soul, as I came to know it better, disgusted me as much as my body.

Certain times were especially dangerous: weekends, the beginning of months (perhaps because I had a little more money—and I had acquired the habit of paid encounters). There are, my dear, such wretched reasons. I also feared the eves of holidays, their idleness, their sadness for those who live alone. I shut myself up on those days: I paced back and forth, tired of seeing my image reflected in the mirror, hating that mirror which inflicted my own presence on me. Dusk began to fill the room. Shadows fell upon things like an additional layer of dust. I did not close the window, because I wanted air; the noises from outside tired me so that I could not think. I was sitting down; I endeavored to fix my mind on some idea, but one idea always leads to another; and one does not know where that will end up. It seemed better to move, to walk about. There is nothing wrong with going out at dusk; and yet it was a defeat which looked forward to another. I loved that hour when the fever of cities throbbed. I shall not describe the hallucinatory quest for pleasure, the potential mortifications, the bitterness of a moral humiliation much worse than the sin itself when no relief comes to compensate it. I shall pass over the somnambulism of desire, the abrupt resolution which sweeps away all others, the alacrity of a body which, finally, no longer obeys anything but itself. We often describe the happiness of a soul which disencumbers itself of its body; there are moments in life when the body disencumbers itself of the soul.

Dear God, when shall I die? . . . Monique, you will remember those words. They are at the beginning of an old German prayer. I am tired of this mediocre being without future, without any faith in the future, of this being I am obliged to call myself, because I cannot separate myself from it. It obsesses me with its sorrows, with its pains; I see it suffer—and I am not even capable of consoling it. I am certainly better than it. I can speak of it as I would of a stranger; I do not understand the reasons that make me its prisoner. And the most terrible thing, perhaps, is that others will know of me only this person struggling with life. It is hardly worth the effort to hope that he will die, since, when he does, I shall die with him. In Vienna, during those years of inner conflict, I often hoped to die.

One does not suffer from one's own vices; one suffers only from not being able to resign oneself to them. I knew all the sophisms of passion; I knew also all the sophisms of conscience. People tell themselves that they disapprove of certain acts because morality is opposed to them; in reality, they obey (they have the good fortune to obey) instinctive loathings. I was struck, despite myself, by the extreme insignificance of our gravest faults, by the tiny place they occupy in our life if our remorse for them does not prolong their duration. Our body forgets like our soul; that is possibly what explains why some of us experience renewals of innocence. I attempted to forget; I almost did. Then, that sort of amnesia appalled me. My memories, which always seemed to me incomplete, tortured me even more. I embraced them in order to bring them to life again. I grew desperate when they paled. I had nothing but them to compensate me for the present, and for the future I had renounced. Having forbidden myself so many things, I no longer had the courage to forbid myself my past.

I triumphed. Through miserable relapses and even more miserable victories, I managed to achieve living a whole year as I would have wished to live my entire life. My dear, do not smile. I do not wish to exaggerate my merit (to claim merit for abstaining from a fault is a form of being guilty). Sometimes one controls one's acts; one controls less often one's thoughts; one never controls one's dreams. I had dreams. I came to know the danger of stagnant waters. It seems that acting absolves us. There is something pure, even in a culpable act, compared to the thoughts we form about it. Or, if you wish, you could say that acts are less impure because of the element of mediocrity reality always possesses. The year in which I did, I assure you, nothing reprehensible was troubled with more obsessions than any other, and with viler ones. One would have said that this wound, closed too quickly, had reopened in the soul and ended up by poisoning it. It would be easy for me to compose a dramatic account, but neither you nor I are interested in dramas—and there are many things that one expresses best by not saying them. And so, I loved life. It was in the name of life, that is to say, my future, that I forced myself to triumph over myself. Yet one hates life when one suffers. I had suicidal obsessions; I had others even more abominable. I saw in the humblest objects of daily life nothing more than the instruments of potential destruction. I was afraid of fabrics, because one can knot them; of scissors, because of their points; above all, of things that could cut. I was tempted by these brutal forms of deliverance: I put a locked drawer between my insanity and myself.

I became hard. Up to that point I had refrained from judging others; I would have ended up, if I had had the strength, by being as pitiless to them as I was to myself. I did not pardon the next man his smallest transgressions; I feared that any indulgence toward someone else would lead me, confronted with my conscience, to excuse my own faults. I was suspicious of the softness provided by sweet sensations; I came to hate nature because of the tenderness of spring. I avoided as much as possible music that moved me: my hands, placed before me on the keys, troubled me with the memory of caresses. I feared the unforeseen in social encounters, the danger in human faces. I was alone. Then my solitude made me afraid. One is never completely alone: unhappily, one is always with oneself.

Music, the joy of the strong, is the consolation of the weak. Music had been an occupation which I took up in order to earn a living. To teach it to children is a painful task, because technique diverts them from the soul. One ought, I think, to give them at the outset a taste of the soul. In any case, the accepted method is opposed to that, and neither my students nor their parents were interested in changing the accepted method. But I preferred children to the older people who came to me and thought they were obliged to express something. Then, too, I was less intimidated by children. Had I tried, I could have had more lessons; the ones I gave were enough for me to live on. As it was, I was working too much. I do not believe in the cult of work when the result matters only to oneself. No doubt, to tire oneself is a way of exerting control over one's own body, but bodily exhaustion ends by numbing the soul. I do not know, Monique, if an unquiet soul is not preferable to a soul asleep.

I still had my evenings. Every evening, I allowed myself a moment of music which was reserved for me alone. To be sure, solitary pleasure is sterile pleasure, yet no pleasure is sterile when it puts our being in harmony with life. Music transports me into a world where grief does not cease to exist but expands and grows quiet, becomes at once calmer and profounder, like a raging river which dissolves into a lake. When you come home late, you cannot sit down to play very loud music; I have never liked it anyway. I realized that the people in the house at best tolerated my music, and no doubt sleep for tired people is worth more than all potential melodies. That is how, my dear, I learned to play almost always very softly, as if I were afraid of awakening something. Silence compensates not only for the impotence of human words, it compensates also for the poverty of musical expression in mediocre musicians. It has always seemed to me that music ought to be nothing more than silence, the mystery of silence seeking to express itself. Consider, for example, a fountain: the mute water fills the pipes, gathers itself together, jets upward, and the pearl that falls creates the sound. It has always seemed to me that music ought to be nothing but the overflow of a great silence.

As a child, I thirsted for fame. At that age we long for fame the way we long for love: we have need of others to show us ourselves. I do not say that ambition is a pointless vice; it can serve to urge on the soul. The only thing is, it exhausts the soul. I know of no success which is not bought with a half lie; I know of no listeners who do not force us either to omit or to exaggerate something. I have often thought with sadness that a truly beautiful soul would not obtain fame because it would not desire it. This idea, which disabused me of fame, also disabused me of genius. I have often thought that genius is only a special eloquence, a formidable gift of expression. Even if I were Chopin, Mozart, or Pergolesi, I would express, imperfectly perhaps, nothing more than what a village musician attempts every day when he does his best in all humility. I did my best. My first concert was something worse than a failure; it was half a success. In order for me to decide to give it at all, I needed material reasons and that authority worldly people assume over us when they want to help us. My family had a number of rather distant relatives in Vienna. They were for me almost protectors, and yet they were complete strangers. My poverty rather humiliated them. They wanted me to become famous so that they would not be embarrassed when people spoke of me. I rarely saw them; they probably disliked me because I never gave them the opportunity to refuse me help. Nevertheless, they did help me. They helped me, I am well aware, in the way that cost them the least; but I do not see, my dear, what right we have to demand generosity.

I recall my entrance upon the scene at my first concert. The attendance was not very large, but it was already too large for me. I was suffocating. I disliked this public for whom art is only a necessary vanity, these composed faces simulating soul, the absence of soul. I found it hard to comprehend that one could play before unknown people, at a fixed hour, for a fee paid in advance. I guessed at the preconceived appreciation they would feel obliged to formulate upon leaving. I detested their fondness for needless overstatement, even the interest that they had in me because I was from their world, and the factitious glitter with which the women garbed themselves. I already preferred the audiences of popular concerts given in the evening in some shabby hall, where I occasionally agreed to play for nothing. People came there in the hope of learning something. They were not necessarily more intelligent than the others; they simply had better motivation. They would, after supper, have dressed themselves as nicely as possible; they would have submitted to being cold, during two long hours, in a concert hall that was almost dark. People who go to the theater seek to forget themselves; those who go to a concert seek rather to find themselves. Between the dispersal of the day and the dissolution of sleep, they steep themselves in what they are. The tired faces of evening audiences, faces which relax into their dreams and seem to bathe there. My face . . . am I not also very poor, I who have neither love nor faith nor admissible desire, I who have only myself to count on, and who am almost always unfaithful to myself?

The following winter was very rainy. I took cold. I was too accustomed to being always slightly ill to worry when I was genuinely ill. During the year of which I speak, I had been afflicted again by the nervous disorders I had known in childhood. The cold I caught, which I did not take care of, weakened me further. I fell ill again, and this time quite seriously.

I understood then the happiness of being alone. Had I died at that time, I would have had no one to miss me. My isolation was absolute. A letter from my brothers had in fact just apprised me that my mother was dead, a month ago already, which made me sad, especially not to have known it earlier; it seemed to me that I had been robbed of several weeks of mourning. I was alone. The local doctor, who had finally been called, soon stopped coming, and my neighbors wore themselves out caring for me. I was content to have it so. I was so tranquil that I did not even experience the need to resign myself. I watched my body struggle, suffocate, suffer. My body wanted to live. It had a faith in life that even I admired. I was almost sorry to have held it in contempt, to have discouraged it, to have punished it so cruelly. When I felt better and was able to quit my bed, my mind, still weak, remained incapable of any lengthy reflection; it was through the agency of my body that the first joys came to me. I perceived once again the almost sacred beauty of bread, the modest ray of sun that warmed my face, and the exhilaration that life caused me. A day finally came when I was able to lean out of an open window. The street I lived on in a suburb of Vienna was somber and gray, but there are moments when one tree rising above a wall is enough to remind us that whole forests exist. That day I had, by means of my entire body, which was astonished to live again, my second revelation of the beauty of the world. You know what the first one was. As I did at the first one, I wept, not so much from happiness or from gratitude; I wept at the idea that life was so simple and would be so easy if we ourselves were only simple enough to accept it.

What I hold against sickness is that it makes renunciation too easy. One believes one is cured of desire, but convalescence is a relapse; and one perceives, always with the same stupefaction, that joy can still make us suffer. During the months that followed, I thought I was still able to look on life with the indifferent eye of the sick. I persisted in thinking that I probably would not live much longer; I forgave myself my faults, just as God no doubt will forgive us after death. I no longer reproached myself for being excessively moved by human beauty; I saw in these faint quivers of the heart the weakness of a convalescent, the excusable confusions of a body which had been, so to speak, made new in the face of life. I took up my lessons again, and my concerts. I had to, because my sickness had been very costly. Almost no one had thought to ask about me, and the people in whose homes I gave lessons did not perceive that I was still very weak. One should not hold that against them. For them I was only a mild young man, apparently very well-behaved, whose lessons were not expensive. It was the only way they saw me, and my absence was simply an inconvenience for them. As soon as I was capable of a longish walk, I went to see Princess Catherine.

At that time the Prince and Princess de Mainau

spent several months each winter in Vienna. I fear, my friend, that their little worldly eccentricities have prevented us from appreciating all that was rare and valuable in those people of that other time. They were the survivors of a world that was more reasonable than ours because it was less burdensome. The prince and princess had that easy affability which, in little things, is an adequate replacement for true kindness. We were slightly related on the female side; the princess recalled having been brought up with my maternal grandmother by German canonesses. She liked to recall this distant intimacy, because she was one of those women who consider that age has an additional nobility. Perhaps her only coquetry consisted in keeping her mind young. The beauty of Catherine de Mainau was by then only a memory; instead of mirrors, she had in her room portraits of herself when she was young. Yet one was aware that she had been beautiful. She had, it was said, inspired intense passions; she herself had felt them; she had had sorrows which she had not borne for long. Her griefs were, I suppose, like her ball gowns, which she put on only once. But she kept them all; thus, she had wardrobes full of memories. You often said, my dear, that Princess Catherine had a soul of lace.

I only occasionally attended her *soirées intimes*, but she always received me well. I felt that she did not have any real attachment for me, nothing more than the absentminded affection of an indulgent old lady. And yet I almost loved her. I loved her slightly puffy hands on which her rings were tight, her tired eyes, and her limpid diction. Like my mother, the princess used that soft, liquid French from the century of Versailles which gives the slightest words the old-fashioned grace of a dead language. I rediscovered with her, as I did later with you, some of my natal speech. She did her best to improve my knowledge of the world; she lent me books of poetry; she chose those that were tender, superficial, and difficult. The Princess de Mainau thought me a correct young man; it was the one fault she did not forgive. She questioned me, laughing, about the young women whom I met at her house; she was surprised that I was not taken with any of them. Her simple questions tortured me. Naturally, she perceived that. She found me shy and younger than my age; I was grateful to her for judging me in that way. There is something reassuring, when one is unhappy and believes oneself very sinful, in being treated like an insignificant child.

She knew that I was very poor. Poverty, like sickness, was something unattractive from which she averted her gaze. For nothing in the world would she have consented to climb five flights. Yet you must not, my dear, be too quick to blame her. She had an infinite delicacy. It was, doubtless, in order not to offend me that she gave me only useless presents; but then, the most useless are the most necessary. When she learned that I was sick, she sent me flowers. Flowers do not mind if you live in squalid surroundings. It was more than I expected from anyone. I did not think there was a single person on earth good enough to send me flowers. At that period, she had a passion for mauve lilacs; thanks to her, my convalescence was redolent. I have told you how sad my room was. Possibly, without the lilacs from Princess Catherine, I should never have had the courage to get well.

When I went to thank her, I was still quite weak. I found her, as usual, working on one of those pieces of needlework she rarely had the patience to complete. My thanks surprised her; she had already forgotten that she had sent me flowers. My dear, that outraged me. The beauty of a gift is diminished when the person who gave it attaches no importance to it. At Princess Catherine's, the shutters were almost always closed; by preference she lived in a perpetual twilight, yet even so, the dusty odor of the street invaded her room. It was apparent that summer was beginning. I thought, with overwhelming fatigue, of all I would have to endure in those four summer months. I imagined the lessons becoming scarcer, the nightly futility of going out in quest of a little fresh air, the nervous irritation, the insomnia—and other dangers, too. I was afraid of getting sick again, or worse than sick; and I ended up complaining aloud that the summer had come so quickly. The Princess de Mainau spent the summer at Wand, on an ancient domain she had inherited. For me, Wand was only a vague name like all places we do not believe we shall ever live in; it took me some time to understand that the princess was inviting me there. She invited me out of pity. She invited me gaily, already putting her mind on choosing a room for me, taking, so to speak, possession of my life until the following autumn. I was ashamed, then, to have looked, by complaining, as though I had hoped for something. I accepted. I lacked the courage to punish myself by refusing, and anyway, my dear, you are well aware that one did not resist Princess Catherine.

I went to Wand planning to spend only three weeks there; I stayed several months. They were long, utterly still months. They flowed by slowly, mechanically, truly imperceptibly. One might say that I was waiting without being aware of it. Life there was ceremonial yet simple at the same time; I enjoyed the peacefulness of this easier existence. I cannot say that Wand reminded me of Woroïno. And yet it gave the same impression of age and peaceful continuance. Wealth seemed to have installed itself in that house long ago, just as poverty had in ours. The Princes de Mainau had always been wealthy; one could therefore not be astonished that they remained so, and even the poor were not upset by it. The prince and princess received a great deal; we lived amid books newly arrived from France, scores open on the piano, and the jingling of harnesses. In those cultured yet frivolous surroundings, intelligence seemed simply an additional luxury. No doubt the prince and princess were not really my friends: they were merely my protectors. Laughing, the prince would call me his musician extraordinaire; in the evening it was expected that I should go to the piano. I was quite aware that one could play for those worldly people only music that was banal, as superficial as the words that had just been spoken; yet there is a certain beauty in those forgotten ariettas.

The months spent at Wand seemed to me one long siesta during which I endeavored not to think. The princess had not wanted me to interrupt my concerts, and so I went off to give a number of them in large German towns. There I found myself confronted with familiar temptations, but they constituted mere incidents. My return to Wand erased even the memory of them; once again I used my terrifying ability to forget. The life of people in society is restricted on the surface to a few agreeable, or at least proper, ideas. It is not even hypocrisy; one simply avoids alluding to whatever would be shocking if expressed. They are quite aware that humiliating realities exist, but they live as if they were not subject to them. It is as if one took one's clothing for one's body. To be sure, I was incapable of so crude an error: I had seen myself naked. What I did, however, was to close my eyes. I was not happy at Wand before you arrived; I was merely dormant. Then you came. Nor was I really happy once you were there. I only imagined the existence of happiness. It was like a summer afternoon's dream.

Before you got there, I knew everything about you that one knows about a young woman—that is to say, not much, and only little things. I had been told that you were very beautiful, that you were wealthy and highly accomplished. No one had told me how kind you were; the princess either was unaware of it or else kindness was for her a superfluous attribute: she thought charm was enough. Many young women are very beautiful; many are also wealthy and highly accomplished; but I had no reason to be interested in all that. Do not be surprised, my dear, that so many descriptions should have been to no avail. In the depths of every perfect being there is something unique which discourages praise. The princess wanted me to admire you in advance, and I therefore assumed that you were less simple than you are. Up to that point, it had not displeased me to play the role of a very modest, retiring guest at Wand. But with you there, it seemed as though they were determined to make me shine. I knew well that I was incapable of that, and new faces always intimidated me. If it had been up to me alone, I should have left before your arrival; but that was impossible. I understand now the motive of the prince and princess for detaining me. I unhappily had around me two old people desirous of providing me with happiness.

My dear, you must pardon Princess Catherine. She knew me so little that she thought I was worthy of you. The princess knew that you were very pious; I myself, before knowing you, had had a timorous sort of infantile piety. To be sure, I was Catholic and you were Protestant, but that mattered so little. The princess assumed that a very old name was enough to compensate for my poverty, and your family also took that attitude. With a certain exaggeration perhaps, Catherine de Mainau lamented my solitary, often difficult life. She was afraid of the vulgar suitors you might have. She considered herself obliged, in some way, to replace your mother and mine. And then, too, she was a relative of mine; in this fashion she wanted to please my family. The Princess de Mainau was sentimental; she liked living in the somewhat mawkish atmosphere of German betrothals; for her, marriage was a drawing-room comedy, sprinkled with emotions and smiles, where happiness arrives in the fifth act. Happiness did not arrive, but perhaps, Monique, you and I are incapable of it; and that is not the fault of Princess Catherine.

I believe I told you that the Prince de Mainau had recounted your history to me. I should say, rather, the history of your parents, because that of young women is wholly interior: their life is a poem before it becomes a drama. I had listened to this story with indifference, like one of those interminable accounts of hunts and travels into which the prince would ramble in the evening after a long dinner. It actually was a tale of travel, since the prince had known your father during an expedition in the French Antilles long ago. Dr. Thiébaut was a celebrated explorer. He had married when he was no longer young; you were born in that part of the world. Subsequently, your father, as a widower, left the islands; you lived with relatives on your father's side in a French province. You grew up in a severe environment, which was nonetheless very affectionate; you had the childhood of a happy little girl. But there is certainly no need, my dear, for me to tell you your own history; you know that much better than I. Day after day, verse by verse, it unfolded for you like a psalm. It is not even necessary for you to recall it. It made you what you are, and your gestures, your voice, your entire self bear witness to this tranquil past.

You arrived at Wand one evening at the end of August. I do not recall very precisely the details of your arrival; I know only that you entered not merely into this German household but also into my life. I remember only that it was already dusk and that the lamps in the vestibule had not yet been lit. It was not your first visit to Wand, and so everything had a certain familiarity for you; everything had a knowledge of you also. It was too dark for me to perceive your features; I realized simply that you were very calm. My dear, women are rarely calm: either they are placid or else they are nervous. You were as serene as a lamp. You spoke familiarly with your hosts; you said only what needed to be said, but you said that perfectly. That evening I was even more timid than usual, enough to discourage even your friendliness. And yet I did not dislike you. Nor did I admire you. You were too distant. Your arrival seemed to me simply somewhat less disagreeable than I had at first feared. You see, my dear, that I am truthful.

I am trying to relive, as precisely as possible, the weeks which led up to our betrothal. Monique, it is not easy. I must avoid words of happiness or love, for, in fact, I did not love you. Yet you became very dear to me. I have told you how sensitive I am to women's sweetness: with you, I experienced a new feeling of confidence and peace. Like me, you loved long walks in the countryside which led nowhere. For me, it was not necessary that they lead anywhere. I was at peace beside you. Your pensive nature harmonized with my timid nature; we were silent together. And then your lovely, grave voice, somewhat subdued, your voice drenched with silence, gently questioned me about my art and myself. I understood already that you felt a sort of tender pity for me. You were a kind person. You knew about suffering from having so often healed or consoled it. You saw in me a young man who was ill or poor. I was indeed so impoverished that I did not love you. I simply found you sweet. I came to imagine that I would have been happy to belong to you: I mean to say, as your brother. I did not go further than that. I was not so presumptuous as to imagine anything more—or, perhaps, my nature kept silence. As I think of it, it seems already a considerable accomplishment for it to have kept silence.

You were very pious. In that period, you and I still believed in God—that is, the God that people depict for us as if they knew Him. And yet you never spoke of Him. Perhaps you thought there was nothing one could say, or else you never spoke of Him because you felt that He was present. One speaks of those one loves especially when they are not there. You lived in God. Like me, you were fond of those old books of the mystics, who seem to have looked into life and death through a crystal. We lent each other books. We read together, but not aloud, aware that words often destroy something. We had two harmonious silences. We waited for each other at the bottom of the page; your finger traced the beginnings of prayers across the lines as if you were showing me a route. One day when I had more courage and you even more tenderness than usual, I admitted to you my fear of being damned. You smiled, gravely, to give me confidence. Suddenly this idea seemed small, mean, and terribly remote: I understood that day the indulgence of God.

Thus, I do have memories of love. No doubt it was not a true passion, but I am not sure whether a true passion would have made me better or only happier. Nevertheless, I see too clearly how much egotism such an emotion contains. I attached myself to you. I attached myself: that, unhappily, is the only appropriate word. Weeks went by; every day the princess found reasons to keep you there longer; I think you began to become accustomed to me. We came to exchange our memories of childhood. Thanks to you, I was aware of happy ones. Through me, you were aware of sad ones. It was as if we had divided our pasts in half. Every hour increased this shy fraternal intimacy, and I realized with horror that we had come to be thought of as fiancés.

I unburdened myself to Princess Catherine. I could not tell her everything: I emphasized the extreme poverty against which my family struggled; you were, unhappily, far too rich for me. Your name alone, celebrated for two generations in the world of learning, was worth more than an impoverished Austrian nobility. Finally, I was bold enough to allude to earlier faults of a serious nature which forbade me your love but which naturally I could not be explicit about. This half confession, painful enough in itself, succeeded only in causing a smile. Monique, I was not even believed. I was colliding with the obstinacy of frivolous people. The princess had once and for all promised herself to unite us in marriage: she had formed a favorable opinion of me which she would not change. The world, which is sometimes too stern, compensates for its harshness with its inattention. Quite simply, one is never suspected. The Princess de Mainau said that experience had made her frivolous: neither she nor her husband took me seriously. My scruples seemed to them to bear witness to a true love; because I was apprehensive, they thought I was being unselfish.

Virtue has its temptations like everything else, far more dangerous because we are not on the lookout for them. Before I knew you, I dreamed of marriage. Perhaps those whose existence is irreproachable dream about something else; in this way we compensate for having but one nature and for living on only one side of happiness. I had never, even in moments of complete abandon, believed that my condition was definitive or even lasting. In my family, I had known admirable examples of feminine tenderness. My religious ideas led me to see in marriage the only blameless and permissible ideal. I came to imagine that a very gentle, very affectionate, very serious young woman might one day teach me to love her. Except at home, I had never known similar young women. I thought of those who smiled pallidly in the pages of old books. Julie von Charpentier or Thérèse de Brunswick. They were rather vague images and, unhappily, very pure ones. In any case, my dear, a dream is not a hope. One makes do with it; one thinks it even sweeter when one believes it impossible, because then one does not have the threat of living it someday.

What should I have done? One does not dare tell everything to a young woman, even when her spirit is already the spirit of a woman. I would have lacked the words; I would have given my acts either a diminished or an exaggerated image. To say everything was to lose you. Had you consented to marry me nonetheless, it would always have cast a shadow over whatever confidence you had in me. I needed that confidence to oblige me, in some way, not to betray it. I believed it was my right (or rather my duty) not to reject the one chance of salvation life gave me. I felt I had come to the end of my courage: I understood that, alone, I should never get well. At that time, I wanted desperately to get well. One tires of living only with the furtive, despised forms of human happiness. With a word, I could have broken our tacit engagement: I could have found excuses; it would have been enough to say that I was not in love with you. I refrained, not because the princess, my sole protector, would never have forgiven me; I refrained because I had hope in you. I let myself slide into . . . I shall not say into this happiness (my dear, we are not happy), but rather into this crime. The desire to behave properly carried me into lower depths than the worst motives: I stole your future. I brought you nothing, not even the great love you counted on. What virtues I had were the accomplices of this lie; and my egotism was as hateful as it deemed itself proper.

You were in love with me. I am not vain enough to believe that you loved me with passion; I continue to ask myself how it was possible not so much that you fell in love with me as that you adopted me in that way. Each of us knows so little about love as other people understand it. For you, love was perhaps only an impassioned kindness. Or else, you were attracted to me. I attracted you precisely because of those good qualities which too often grow in the shade of our worst faults: weakness, indecision, subtlety. Above all, you felt sorry for me. I had been imprudent enough to inspire pity in you. Because you had been good to me for several weeks, you thought it would be natural to be so for the rest of your life: you thought it was enough to be perfect in order to be happy. I thought it enough, in order to be happy, not to be guilty any longer.

We were married at Wand one rainy day in October. Perhaps, Monique, I might have wished our engagement had been longer; I like to be borne along, not dragged, by the passage of time. I was not without anxieties about the existence which opened before me: remember that I was twenty-two years old and you were the first woman who preoccupied my life. But, with you beside me, everything was always very simple. I was so grateful to you for frightening me so little. The guests at the castle departed one after the other. We were going to depart also, together. We were married in the village church, and since your father had gone off on one of his distant expeditions, we had with us only some friends and my brother. My brother had come even though the trip was expensive; he thanked me almost effusively for having, as he put it, saved our family. I was aware that he was alluding to your fortune, and that filled me with shame. I did not answer. And yet, my dear, would I have been more culpable in sacrificing you to my family than in sacrificing you to myself? I remember that it was one of those days of intermittent sun and rain which, like a human face, easily change expression. It seemed to me that the day was trying to be fine and that I was trying to be happy. My God, I *was* happy. Timorously happy.

And here, Monique, there should be silence. Here my dialogue with myself should cease: here begins the dialogue of two united souls and bodies—united, or merely joined. To say everything, my dear, would require an audacity I forbid myself; above all, it would be necessary for me to be a woman as well. I would merely compare my memories with yours, relive, in a sort of slow motion, those moments of sadness or of painful joy that we lived out perhaps too hastily. All that comes back to me like vanished thoughts, like shy, whispered confidences, like very soft music you have to listen to in order to hear it. Let me see if it is not possible also to write in whispers.

My health, which was still precarious, worried you all the more since I did not complain about it. You were resolved that we should spend our first months together in milder climates: the very day of our marriage, we set out for Merano. Subsequently, winter drove us toward even warmer lands; I saw for the first time the sea, and the sea bathed in sunlight. But that is unimportant. On the contrary, I should have preferred other regions, sadder, more austere, which harmonized with the existence that I was determined to wish to live. Those carefree countries of bodily happiness caused me distress and confusion; I was always suspicious that joy contained a sin. The more my conduct seemed reprehensible to me, the more I clung to rigorous moral standards which condemned my acts. Our theories, Monique, when they are not the formulation of our instincts, are the defenses with which we oppose our instincts. I was annoyed at you for making me notice the deep red heart of a rose, a statue, the dusky beauty of a passing child; I experienced a sort of ascetic horror at these innocent things. For the same reason, I should have preferred you to be less beautiful.

We had put off, with a sort of tacit understanding, the moment when we would be completely each other's. I thought about it in advance with some disquiet, with revulsion also; I feared that so great an intimacy was going to spoil or debase something. Then, too, one never knows what the sympathies or antipathies of the body will bring about between two people. Doubtless, such ideas were not very healthy, but nevertheless those are the ideas I had. Every evening, I would ask myself whether I dared join you. My dear, I did not dare. Finally, I really had to: otherwise, you surely would not have understood. I think, with a certain sadness, how much more another person would have appreciated the beauty—the goodness—of that gift, so utterly simple, of yourself. I would not wish to say anything which might risk shocking you, even less making you smile, but it seems to me that it was a maternal gift. Later, when I saw your child nestle against you, I thought that every man, without knowing it, seeks in women above all the memory of the time when his mother embraced him. That, at least, is the case for me. I recall with infinite pity your rather troubled efforts to reassure me, to console me, perhaps to cheer me up; and I almost think I was your first child.

I was not happy. I felt, of course, a certain disappointment in this lack of happiness, but in the end I resigned myself to it. In some fashion, I had renounced happiness, or at least joy. And then I told myself that the first months of a marriage are rarely the sweetest, that two people, abruptly joined by life, cannot so rapidly absorb themselves into each other and become truly one. That requires a great deal of patience and good will. We had both. I told myself, with even greater justice, that we are not owed any joy, and that it is wrong for us to complain. Everything would seem better, I suppose, if we were reasonable, and happiness is perhaps only an unhappiness which is better tolerated. I told myself that, because courage consists in accepting things when we cannot change them. And yet, if there is something lacking in life, or merely in ourselves, it is not any less significant, and we suffer from it just as much. And you, too, my dear, you were not happy either.

You were twenty-four years old. That was, roughly, the age of my older sisters. But, unlike them, you were not withdrawn or shy: you possessed an admirable vitality. You were not born for an existence of small sorrows or little happinesses; you were too powerful. As a young girl, you had conceived an idea of your married life which was exceedingly severe and grave, an ideal of tenderness more affectionate than loving. Nevertheless, without being aware of it yourself, into the strict routine of those dull and often difficult duties which, according to you, were to comprise your whole future, you inserted something else. Custom does not permit women passion: it permits them only love, and that is perhaps why they love so completely. I dare not say that you were born for a life of pleasure; there is something in that word which is sinful, or at least forbidden; I should rather say, my dear, that you were born to know and to give joy. One must endeavor to become sufficiently pure to encompass all the innocence of joy, that sun-drenched form of happiness. You had thought that giving it would be enough to get it back in return. I do not claim that you were disappointed: it takes a great deal of time for a woman's feeling to change itself into thought: you were merely sad.

So, I did not love you. You gave up asking me for the great love that, I have no doubt, will never be inspired in me by any woman, since I could not feel it for you. But you were unaware of that. You were too reasonable not to resign yourself to such a trapped life, but you were also too healthy not to suffer from it. But one is the last to perceive the suffering one causes. Moreover, you hid it; at the beginning, I thought you were almost happy. You endeavored to dress in a manner that would please me; you wore heavy clothes which hid your beauty, because you already understood that the slightest effort to adorn yourself frightened me, as if it were an offer of love. Without loving you, I was overcome with a sort of anguished affection for you; your absence, even for a moment, saddened me for an entire day, and one could not have said whether I suffered from being away from you or whether, quite simply, I was afraid of being alone. Even I did not know. And then, also,

I was afraid to be together with you, to be together and alone with you. I smothered you with an atmosphere of nervous tenderness; I would ask you, twenty times in a row, if you cared for me; I knew only too well that that was impossible.

We forced ourselves to practice a sort of heightened religious devotion, which really did not correspond at all to our true beliefs: those who lack everything else turn to God, and at that moment God, too, abandons them. Often we lingered on in those dark, welcoming old churches one visits in foreign countries; we even acquired the habit of going there to pray. We would return in the evening, pressed against one another, united at least by a mutual fervor; we would invent pretexts for remaining in the street to watch the life of other people: the life of others always seems easier to us, because we do not have to live it. We were too well aware that, somewhere, our room was awaiting us, a transient room, bleak, naked, vainly open to the warm Italian nights, a room without solitude and, at the same time, without intimacy. For we shared the same room, and it was I who wished it so. Every evening, we hesitated to light the lamp; its light bothered us, and yet we were not able to extinguish it, either. You found me pale; you were no less so; I was afraid you had caught cold; you gently reproached me for having tired myself with excessively long prayers: we had for each other a desperate sort of benevolence. You suffered at that time from intolerable insomnia; I, too, had trouble getting to sleep; we both pretended to sleep in order not to be obliged to complain to each other. Or else you wept. You wept as noiselessly as possible so that I would not be aware of it, and I pretended not to hear you. It is perhaps better not to notice tears when there is nothing one can do to console them.

My character changed. I become moody, difficult, irritable; it seemed as though one virtue had given me dispensation from the others. I became vexed with you for not succeeding in giving me the calm I had counted on and which was, dear God, all that I asked for. I acquired the habit of semi-confidences; I tortured you with confessions all the more distressing in that they were incomplete. We found in tears a sort of miserable satisfaction; our mutual unhappiness managed to bring us together as much as happiness. You, too, changed. It seemed I had robbed you of your former serenity without managing to appropriate it for myself. Like me, you had impatiences and sudden sadnesses, impossible to understand; we became no more than two invalids leaning on each other.

I had completely abandoned music. Music was a part of the world in which I was resigned never to live again. They say that music is the realm of the soul; that may be, my dear: it simply proves that soul and flesh are not separable, that one contains the other, the way a keyboard contains sounds. The silence which follows music is not at all like ordinary silences: it is a heedful silence; it is a living silence. Many unsuspected things whisper within us through this silence, and we never know what the piece of music that has ended is going to tell us. A painting, a statue, even a poem, gives us precise ideas which usually take us no further, but music speaks to us of limitless possibilities. It is dangerous to expose oneself to emotions in art when one has resolved to abstain from them in life. Therefore, I ceased to play and to compose. I am not one of those who ask of art the compensation of pleasure; I love the one and the other, but not the one for the other—these two rather sad forms of all human desire. I no longer composed. My revulsion against life gradually extended to those dreams of an ideal life; for a work of art, Monique, is a dream of life. That simple joy which the achievement of a work of art gives every artist dried up within me, or perhaps it is more accurate to say that it froze within me. That was perhaps the result of the fact that you were not a musician: my renunciation, my fidelity, would not have been complete if I had participated every evening in a world of harmony which you could not enter. I ceased to work. I was poor; until my marriage, I had had difficulty making an adequate living. Now I discovered a sort of voluptuousness in depending on you, even on your fortune. This rather humiliating situation was a sort of guarantee against the old sin. We all,

Monique, have certain strange assumptions. It is merely cruel to deceive a woman who loves us, but it would be hateful to be unfaithful to one on whose money we live. And you, so cautious, did not dare blame me openly for my complete inactivity. You feared that I would see in your words a criticism of my poverty.

The winter, then the spring, went by. Our excesses of grief had worn us out as much as a great debauch. We came to know that aridity in the heart which follows excessive tears, and my dejection seemed like calmness. I was almost terrified to feel myself so calm; I believed that I had triumphed over myself. One is always so ready, alas, to become disgusted with one's own triumphs. We attributed our despondency to the exhaustion of traveling; and so we took up residence in Vienna. I felt a certain repugnance in coming back to that city where I had lived alone. But you, with tender delicacy, were determined not to take me too far away from my own country. I tried to believe that I would be less unhappy in Vienna than I had been before; but, above all, I was less free. I let you choose the furnishings and the curtains for our rooms; with a certain bitterness, I watched you coming and going in those still-empty rooms in which our two existences would be imprisoned. Viennese society was taken with your dark, pensive beauty: the social world, which neither you nor I were used to, gave us a little time to forget how alone we were. But then we tired of it. We developed a kind of determination to endure boredom in that house which was too new, whose objects had no memories for us, whose mirrors did not know us. My effort at virtue and your attempt at love did not even manage to serve as a distraction for us.

Everything, even a moral failure, has its advantages for a mind that is even faintly lucid; it provides a less conventional view of the world. My less solitary life and my reading of books taught me the difference that exists between external conformity and inner morality. Men do not say the whole truth about themselves, but when, like me, one has been forced into the habit of certain reticences, one very quickly perceives that they are universal. I had acquired a singular aptitude for guessing hidden vices or weaknesses. My conscience, stripped naked, revealed to me the conscience of others. No doubt, those with whom I compared myself would have been indignant at such a comparison. They thought of themselves as normal, perhaps because their vices were so ordinary; nonetheless, could I deem them truly superior to me, in their search for pleasure which culminated only in itself and which, most often, did not envisage a child? I was finally able to tell myself that my only mistake (or, rather, my only unhappiness) was to be, certainly not worse than everyone, but only different. And yet many people accommodate themselves to instincts like mine; it is neither so rare nor so strange. I hated myself for having tragically accepted precepts which so many examples contradict—and human morality is nothing more than one great compromise. Dear God, I blame no one. Everyone broods in silence over his own secrets and dreams, without ever admitting them, even to himself, and everything would be made plain if one did not lie. Thus, I had tortured myself with very little cause. Having conformed to the strictest rules of morality, I now gave myself the right to judge them. And one could say that my thoughts dared to be freer from the very moment when I abandoned all freedom in my life.

I have not yet said how much you wanted a son. I, too, passionately wanted one. Nevertheless, when I knew that we were to have a child I felt very little joy. No doubt, childless marriage is only an allowed debauch. If a woman's love merits a respect which a man's does not, that is perhaps only because it contains a future. But it is not at the moment when life seems absurd and deprived of any goal that one can rejoice in perpetuating it. The child we had dreamed of together was going to come into the world among two strangers: he was neither the proof nor the fulfillment of happiness, but its compensation. We vaguely hoped that everything would be all right as soon as he was there, and I had wanted him because you were sad. At first, you even felt some shyness in speaking to me of him; that, more than anything else, shows how much our lives had remained distant. And yet this tiny being began to help us. I thought of him rather as if he were the child of someone else. I savored the sweetness of our intimacy which had once again become fraternal and no longer required any passion. It seemed to me that you were virtually my sister, or some near relative who had been entrusted to me and whom I had to take care of, reassure, and perhaps console for an absence. You grew to love enormously this little creature who was already alive, at least for you. My own contentment, which was so apparent, was not stripped of egotism either: not having known how to make you happy, I found it natural to hope that the child would bring you happiness.

Daniel was born in June at Woroïno in the melancholy countryside of the Montagne Blanche where I myself had been born. We were eager that he should come into the world in this landscape of the past: for you, it was a way of giving me more completely my son. The house, even though restored and newly painted, was the same as ever: it seemed merely to have become much larger, only because we were so many fewer. My brother (I had only one brother left) lived there with his wife. They were very provincial people whom solitude had made uncouth and poverty fearful. They welcomed you with a rather awkward eagerness, and as the trip had tired you, they offered you the honor of the large bedroom where my mother had died and we had been born.

Your hands, resting on the whiteness of the sheets, looked almost like hers; every morning, as in the days when I used to come in to see my mother, I waited for those long, fragile fingers to be placed on my head in blessing. But I could not ask for such a thing: I contented myself with simply kissing them. And yet I had such great need of that blessing. The room was rather dark, with a state bed hung with heavy curtains. I imagine that many women of my family in times past had lain there to await their child or their death—and death is perhaps nothing more than giving birth to a soul.

The last weeks of your pregnancy were painful. One evening, my sister-in-law came and told me that I should pray for you. I did not pray. I simply told myself over and over again that you were doubtless going to die. I was afraid of not feeling a sufficiently sincere despair: I felt, in advance, a sort of remorse. What is more, you were resigned to dying. You were resigned in the way people are when they do not especially care to go on living: in your placidity I saw a reproach. Perhaps you felt that our marriage was not destined to last for a lifetime and that you would end up loving someone else. When one is afraid of the future, it makes death seem easy. I held your hands, which were always slightly feverish, in mine. We both refrained from speaking in the presence of the mutual thought that you would quite possibly die; and you were so exhausted that you did not even ask what would become of the child. I told myself, in rebellion, that nature is unjust to those who obey her clearest laws, since every birth imperils two lives. Everyone causes suffering when he is born, and suffers when he dies. But that life is dreadful is nothing; what is worse is that it is vain and without beauty. The solemnity of a birth, like that of a death, is lost in repulsive or merely commonplace details for those who are in attendance. I was no longer admitted into your room: you struggled amid the cares and prayers of women, and since the lamps remained lighted all night, one was aware that someone was expected. Your cries, when I heard them beyond the closed doors, were almost inhuman and horrified me. I had never dreamed in advance that you would have to come to grips with such an animal form of suffering, and I hated this child who made you scream. Monique, one emotion leads to another, not only in everyday life, but within the depths of the soul also: the memory of those hours when I thought you were lost seems to have brought me back to where my instincts had always drawn me.

I was ushered into your room to see the child. Now everything had become peaceful again; you were happy, but with a physical happiness comprised chiefly of fatigue and liberation. The child, however, was crying in the arms of the women. I suppose he suffered from the cold, from the noise of words, from the hands which took care of him, from the touch of the swaddlings. Life had snatched him away from the warm maternal shadows. He was afraid, I think, and nothing—not even night, not even death—would ever replace for him that truly primordial refuge, for death and night have cold shadows and are not animated by the beating of a heart. I felt so shy before that child I was supposed to embrace. He inspired in me not tenderness, nor even affection, but a great pity; for one does not ever know in the presence of newborn infants what cause for tears the future will give them.

I told myself that he would be yours—your child, Monique, much more than mine. He would inherit from you not only the fortune so long missing from Woroïno (and while a fortune, my dear, does not give happiness, it often makes it possible) but also your lovely, calm gestures, your intelligence, and that radiant smile which greets us in French paintings. At least I hoped this would be the case. With some blind feeling of duty I had made myself responsible for his life, which ran considerable risk of not being happy since he was my son, and my only saving grace had been to give him an admirable mother. Nevertheless, I told myself that he was a Géra, that he belonged to that family in which the members passed on, as if they were precious jewels, thoughts so ancient that no one has them any more, like gilded sleighs and court carriages. He was descended, like me, from Polish, Podolian, and Bohemian ancestors.

He would have their passions, their sudden depressions, their taste for sadness and bizarre pleasures, all their fate together with my own. For we come from a very curious race, where madness and melancholy alternate from century to century like black eyes and blue eyes. Daniel and I have blue eyes. The child was sleeping now in the cradle placed next to the bed, and the lamps which had been put on the table illuminated things indistinctly, including the family portraits, which one usually does not notice since one has seen them so often. But now these portraits ceased to be a presence and became an apparition. Thus, the will those ancestral figures expressed had been realized: our marriage had produced a child. By means of him, this ancient race would prolong itself into the future, and it was now of little importance whether my own existence continued. I no longer interested the dead, and I in turn could disappear, die, or else begin again to live.

The birth of Daniel did not bring us any closer together: it disappointed us as much as love had. We did not take up again our shared existence; I had ceased to nestle against you at night like a child who has fear of the dark, and I took back the room where I slept when I was sixteen years old. In that bed, where I found, along with my past dreams, the hollow my body had formerly made, I had the sense of rejoining myself. My dear, we are wrong to think that life changes us; it wears us away, and that which it wears away in us are the things we have learned. I had not changed; it was just that events had interposed themselves between me and my own nature. I was what I had always been, perhaps more profoundly so than before, because to the extent that we lose one after another our illusions and our beliefs, we come to know better our true being. So many efforts and so much good will ended in my discovering that I was what I had always been: a rather troubled soul, whom two years of virtue had disillusioned. Monique, that is disheartening. The long maternal labor which had been accomplished in you seemed to bring your nature back to its pristine simplicity: you were, as you had been before marriage, a young person who wished for happiness, yet steadier now, calmer, and less burdened with soul. Your beauty had acquired a sort of abundant peace; it was I, now, who knew that I was ill, and I congratulated myself for it. A sense of shame will always prevent me from telling you how many times during those summer months I desired to die; nor do I wish to know if, when you compared yourself to happier women, you held it against me for having ruined your future. And yet we loved each other, as much as one can love without any passion for each other; the summer (it was the second since our marriage) was coming to an end a little hastily, as summers do in northern countries. We managed to savor in silence the end of a summer and of an affection, both of which had borne fruit and now had only to die. It was in the midst of this sadness that music came back to me.

One September evening, the night before our return to Vienna, I surrendered to the attraction of the piano, which up to then had remained closed. I was alone in the drawing room, which was almost dark, and it was, as I have said, my last evening at Woroïno. For several long weeks, a physical disquiet had entered into me, a fever, and an insomnia which I fought against and which I attributed to the autumn. There is a moist, cool sort of music in which one can quench one's thirst, or at least so I thought. I began to play. I played. At first I played with caution, softly, delicately, as if I were trying to put my soul to sleep. I had chosen the calmest pieces, pure mirrors of thought, Debussy or Mozart, and one would have said, as they did formerly in Vienna, that I was afraid of emotional music. Yet my soul, Monique, did not wish to sleep. Or perhaps it was not even the soul. I played vaguely, allowing each note to float over the silence. It was, as I have already said, my last evening at Woroïno. I knew that my hands would never again touch those keys, that this room would never again, because of me, be filled with music. I interpreted my physical ailments as a foreboding of death: I was resolved to let myself die. Abandoning my soul on the crest of arpeggios like a body on a wave when the wave breaks, I waited for the music to ease me toward the next descent into the abyss of oblivion. I played, overwhelmed. I told myself that I had to remake my life and that nothing, not even healing, could heal me. I felt too tired for such a succession of setbacks and efforts, both of them exhausting, and yet I was already taking pleasure, through the music, in my weakness and my surrender. I was no longer able, as I once had been, to despise the life of passion, even though I was afraid of it. My soul was more deeply embedded in my flesh, and what I regretted as I climbed back, from thought to thought, from musical phrase to musical phrase, toward my most intimate and least admitted past was not my transgressions but those opportunities for joy I had rejected. What I regretted was not having given in too often, but rather for too long and with too much vigor having struggled not to give in.

I played in despair. The human soul is slower than we are: that makes me admit that it may also be more durable. It is always a little behind our current life. I was only beginning to comprehend the meaning of my inner music, the music of joy and savage desire that I had stifled within me. I had reduced my soul to one single melody, plaintive and monotonous; I had filled my life with a silence out of which only psalms were permitted to rise. I do not have sufficient faith, my dear, to limit myself to psalms, and if I repent, it is of my repentance. Sounds, Monique, spread out into time like forms in space, and until a piece of music has ceased, it remains in part plunged in the future. There is something very moving for the improviser in the choice of which note will follow. I began to comprehend that liberty both art and life have when they obey only the laws of their own development. The rhythm followed the rise of my inner anguish; the auscultation is terrible when the heart beats too rapidly. What was now born out of the instrument in which my real self had been locked up for two years was no longer a chant of sacrifice, or even of desire, or of joy so near. It was hate: hate for everything that had falsified me and crushed me for so long. With a sort of cruel pleasure, I realized that you could hear me playing from your room: I told myself that that was sufficient as a confession and an explanation.

And it was at that moment that I noticed my hands. My hands rested on the keys, two naked hands without rings on them—it was as if I saw my soul before my eyes, twice alive. My hands—and I can speak of them because they are my only friends—seemed to me all at once extraordinarily sensitive; even motionless, they seemed to stroke the silence as if to arouse it to manifest itself in chords. They were at rest, still trembling somewhat from the rhythm, and in them were contained all future deeds, just as all possible sounds sleep within the piano. They had encircled bodies in the brief joy of embraces; they had touched, on resonant keyboards, the form of invisible notes; they had, in the dark, traced with a caress the contours of sleeping bodies. Often I had held them uplifted in an attitude of prayer; often I had joined them with yours; but of all that they no longer had any memory. They were anonymous hands, the hands of a musician. They were, by means of music, my intermediary with that infinite being we are tempted to call God, and, by their caresses, my means of contact with the life of other people. They were etiolated, as pale as the ivory on which they rested, for I had deprived them of sunshine, or of work, and of joy. And yet they remained faithful servants; they had provided me with nourishment when music was my only livelihood; and I began to understand that there is a certain beauty in living from one's art, since it frees us from everything that is not itself. My hands, Monique, were to liberate me from you. They would once again reach out without constraint; they would open for me, these liberating hands, the doors of departure. Doubtless, my dear, it is absurd to tell you everything, but that evening, awkwardly, the way one seals a pact with oneself, I kissed my two hands.

I shall pass quickly over the following days, when my feelings concern and move only me. I prefer to keep for myself my intimate memories, since I can speak to you only with a discretion which might appear to be born of shame, and because I would be lying if I were to show repentance. Nothing is sweeter than a defeat one knows to be total: in Vienna, during those last sunlit days of autumn, I knew the wonder of discovering once again my body. My body, which cured me from having a soul. You perceived in me only the fears, the remorse, and the scruples of conscience, not even my own conscience, but that of others which I accepted as guides. I neither knew how nor dared to tell you what ardent adoration made it possible for me to experience the beauty and the mystery of bodies, nor how each of them, when it offered itself, seemed to bestow on me a fragment of human youth. My dear, it is very difficult to live. I have constructed enough moral theories not to construct other contradictory ones: I am too reasonable to believe that happiness exists only in tandem with sin; and vice no more than virtue can give joy to those who do not have joy within themselves. Nevertheless, I much prefer sin (if that is what it is) to a denial of self which leads to self-destruction. Life has made me what I am, the prisoner if you will of instincts which I did not choose but to which I resign myself; and this acquiescence will, I hope, procure me, if not happiness, at least peace. My dear, I have always known you were capable of comprehending everything—which is much rarer than forgiving everything.

And now I bid you farewell. I think, with infinite tenderness, of your womanly, or rather motherly, goodness: I leave you with regret, but I envy your child. You are the only person toward whom I judge myself guilty, yet writing of my life confirms me in my being; I end by grieving for you without severely condemning myself. I have betrayed you; I have not wished to deceive you. You are one of those who always choose, out of duty, the straitest and the hardest way: I would not, by begging for your pity, give you a pretext for further sacrifice. Not having known how to live according to common morality, I endeavor at least to be in harmony with my own: it is precisely when one rejects all principles that one must arm oneself with scruples. I undertook imprudent obligations toward you to which life refused to subscribe. With the utmost humility, I ask you now to forgive me, not for leaving you, but for having stayed so long.

Lausanne
31 August 1927–17 September 1928

Translator's Note

Each successive version of this translation has been painstakingly reviewed by Mme Yourcenar herself, who understood from the outset the special challenges that confront any attempt to render into another idiom the luminous purity of language and the haunting tone of voice which so distinguish her earliest novel. Throughout, she has offered subtle suggestions and poetic solutions. I am deeply grateful to her for her generous collaboration and her unfailing encouragement, but even more for the affectionate friendship she has shared with me for more than a decade now.

Three other close friends, George P. Savidis, Walter C. Hughes, and Jess N. Taylor, were kind enough to read and comment on an early draft, each bringing to it his own astute stylistic sensibility; I am obliged to them for saving me from a number of careless infelicities.

This English version of *Alexis* is dedicated by the

translator, with boundless and abiding love, to its only begetter and to Sheila La Farge.

W.K.

La Perla
Poros (Troezeneas)
July 1983